"Sharon is an inspiring woman wh[...] person of Jesus Christ' to her children and grandchildren. She herself has personally experienced God's unconditional love. In her new book, you will enjoy reading of the Amish community and rural Indiana, which create the setting of an inspirational story and reflect Sharon's own memories. You will be encouraged and inspired to know God in a more intimate relationship and make a difference in the lives around you."

Shelly Diehm

"Only an author with extraordinary compassion would write such a compelling story that touches the human heart. You will be inspired and moved to experience the power of compassion and the transcending values of life. This timely story is right on target to refocus on what really matters. You will be moved and changed by Collie, and you will want to share her story with others."

Kent R. Hunter
Author, *Discover Your Windows:*
Lining Up With God's Vision

"Sharon Hammel, like myself, met the Lord as an adult. Since that time, her desire is to live each day for Him. Her joy of writing has led her to write a beautiful work of fiction about a young lady who also loves the Lord. The story shows us how those who know the Lord also know to include Him in their life as they live to serve using their special gifts."

Deborah Owen
Retired teacher

"This book shows an intimacy of Amish life that is rare, a story that made me laugh out loud, shed a tear, and turn page after page. Easy to love!"

Mark Schuyler
Production reviews
Paramount Pictures

"Sharon Hammel is a dedicated, committed follower of Jesus Christ, using her gifts and abilities to serve Him. She has a deep compassion for people, especially those who are hurting in some way. Her desire is that other people know the same love of God that she enjoys, and I see this book as one of her ways of sharing her faith, and trying to help others see how a relationship with God can change their lives – now and for eternity."

Rev. Paul B. Griebel
Senior Pastor
St. John Lutheran Church
Kendallville, Indiana

"The heart of God lives in the author of this story. God's compassion for those He loves, especially those who face hardships and disadvantages in life, shines through. Sharon also reveals how that same God is the answer to life's mysteries; in ways we can understand and in ways we can't."

Rev. Dr. Robert W. Shriner

"Sharon Hammel has been a Parkview Hospice volunteer for nearly five years. Her primary role has been visiting patients. She has an open, welcoming presence that reflects the relationship she has with the Lord. Her quick smile and gentle manner are a great gift to our Hospice patients."

Mauna Cowan
Hospice Volunteer Coordinator

Handicap Never!
I Will Love You Forever

Sharon Kurtz Hammel

Inspiring Voices books may be ordered through booksellers or by contacting:

Inspiring Voices
1663 Liberty Drive
Bloomington, IN 47403
www.inspiringvoices.com
1-(866) 697-5313

Because of the dynamic nature of the Internet, any web addresses or links contained in this book may have changed since publication and may no longer be valid. The views expressed in this work are solely those of the author and do not necessarily reflect the views of the publisher, and the publisher hereby disclaims any responsibility for them.

Any people depicted in stock imagery provided by Thinkstock are models, and such images are being used for illustrative purposes only.

Certain stock imagery © Thinkstock.

ISBN: 978-1-4624-0435-3 (sc)
ISBN: 978-1-4624-0436-0 (e)

Library of Congress Control Number: 2012922095

Printed in the United States of America

Inspiring Voices rev. date: 11/28/2012

This book is dedicated to the glory of Jesus Christ,
who has loved and blessed me beyond comprehension.

Acknowledgements

To my parents, D.C. and Gertrude Kurtz, who always told us we can be the best at what we want to be.

To my husband, Larry Hammel, thank you for your encouragement and always being in my court in anything I attempt to do.

To my children Vikki Marti, Cathy Michelbrink, and Jack Felger, and my step-children Laura Bailey, Jim Hammel, and Bill Hammel. You are all incredible! Even though you always wondered what I was up to, you always believed in me!

To my very special brother Jack Kurtz, whose death during this writing set me back a few months. He was my rock!

To my brother Earl Lynn Kurtz, what an encourager! Thank you for your tireless help in the preparation and organization of this book.

To my brother Terry Kurtz, what a source of help with information. You are great!

To my three sisters: Norma Boszor, Margaret Newman, and Sue Ziebell. Had they lived, they would have been there all the way for me, as they were during our lives together growing up.

Shelly Hinkley, you are the best! Hours of proofreading is an inexhaustible effort that makes me look good. Bless you!

I saved you for last, Lewis Lambright, because you were a wealth of knowledge and inspiration! You will never be last. Thank you!

All of you are my life's blessings and your sustaining strength encourages me.

Sharon Kurtz Hammel

Contents

Chapter 1

An Orphan

I am blind in one eye and a deaf mute in a world of noises. I do not know who my father was, but I know my birth mother is now living in a nursing home. I presently have no one in my life. February 16, 1957, I was born into a world of silence. My name is Collette Collins. I like to be called Collie!

I was left on the frigid, icy steps of a faded, red, and dingy brick building. The name of the building is "The School for the Deaf." It is located in Indianapolis, Indiana.

Due to my handicap, I was placed in a foster care home. But, when they realized the extent of my handicap — deafness, muteness, and partial blindness — they made the decision not to keep me.

During the next three years, I was placed in five other foster homes with the same results. My handicap was too much to deal with. Up until this point, all the other foster homes were a way station to something more permanent. I did not know, but later learned, that nearly all children up to the age of 12 would be easily adoptable. But these were children who did not have special needs. I could never be matched or comfortable with anyone who speaks. I didn't believe I would ever be adopted and, in fact, became more isolated and did not try in any way to communicate.

When I was 12, I was placed in the home of the Collins' family: Steve and Karen, and their "normal," adopted children, Bobby and Rita. Bobby was 14 years old and very pleasant to look at. He was tall for his age and had blond hair and blue/green eyes. Rita was 10 years old and a brat. Several months later, they elected to adopt me. I felt extremely privileged! There was never a shortage of adoptable children.

We lived in a large, three-bedroom, two-story home in Indianapolis, Indiana. Steve and Karen's bedroom was downstairs with an adjoining bathroom. Bobby had an upstairs bedroom with a walk-in bathroom and shower. Rita and I shared an upstairs bedroom with a small, shared bathroom. Rita did not enjoy sharing and wanted her way about everything. Needless to say, she was very difficult. The kitchen was large with what they called an island in the center. We often ate breakfast there. The living room was large, too. It had two couches, three chairs, end tables, and an ottoman Steve claimed as his. Tree lamps and a piano were along one wall. It also had dingy, yellow and bold wallpaper. Other walls were painted pale yellow. A picture that reminded me of Indianapolis winters hung on one of the walls. It showed a lot of snow and frozen icicles, which made me shiver to look at. We had a small black-and-white television in the living room, where we often gathered in the evenings, reading and eating popcorn.

Rita and I were assigned the job of doing dishes every night, and we would take turns setting the supper table. She always mimicked me when I looked at her. Typical Rita! Bobby was assigned the task of taking out the trash and, during the winter months, shoveling snow. During the summer months he mowed the lawn and, in the fall, raked leaves. We would sometimes rake leaves into piles and then jump in them, scattering leaves everywhere, only to rake them all up again. We had fun and I loved smelling the leaves and smoke coming out of the chimneys around us.

Karen would sometimes play the piano. I could tell she played well because Steve, Bobby, and Rita would shake their bodies to the music and smile. I couldn't hear the music but could see them dance and shake and knew it made everyone happy.

Most of the time, I didn't think Bobby and Rita liked me very well because I could read their lips and they would say, "Collie is deaf and dumb."

I remember lip reading these same words many times before in previous foster care homes. I know I am deaf! I also know I am not dumb! I have become very good at reading lips, partially due to watching television. I realized later I also learned lip reading for survival, because children can be cruel. I know because I have been the object of their cruelty! I was especially hurt receiving notes making fun of me so many times. Adults can hurt even more; they are just more subtle about it.

It appears that love can be somewhat conditional so I try to stay out of everyone's way. Yet, I really want to communicate! I sometimes make gurgling sounds, which can be offensive to a hearing person. No one was more frustrated by that than I! I could see people wherever I went turn away from me in disgust. Even my previous foster parents and families did not demonstrate attention towards me, not even a hug. I floundered like a fish out of water watching everyone in the home talking to one another, lips moving,

laughing, and hugging. Oftentimes I craved to have someone wrap their arms around me and really hug me. Steve and Karen hugged Bobby and Rita. They just could not hug me. I don't know what was wrong and often wondered why they chose to adopt me.

During Christmas 1973 I was almost 17 years old. I received some nice gifts: earrings and two books, which I really wanted. One was *Pilgrim's Progress*. I also opened a gift that contained a pair of gloves and a crocheted hat. I especially liked those, as they were handmade. I knew Karen had worked a long time to make them, because I would see her working at night. I just didn't realize they were for me.

Bobby got a guitar and he was so excited. I read Karen's lips and she said he will drive us all crazy. I sat with him hour after hour watching him play, acting like I loved it. I was the best audience he could have. Little did he remember I was deaf and could not hear him!

Rita received puzzles, two books, a necklace, and socks. She also got crocheted hats and gloves. Steve received a new shirt, socks, and a pair of boots. Karen was delighted with new pots and pans. She also received a pretty blue dress. The color made her eyes stand out beautifully – almost the same color as her dress. Karen was an attractive woman. Her hair was shoulder length, light brown, and parted on the side. Sometimes I was happy she was my foster mother.

Our Christmas dinner consisted of ham, tossed salad, baked potatoes, and apple pie, with ice cold milk for the children and coffee for Steve and Karen.

It was a custom on Christmas Eve for Karen to play the piano. Many of their friends and relatives came to see us and they all gathered around the piano to sing carols. My deafness prevented me from hearing the music, but I could feel the vibration around me and under my feet. These precious moments allowed me freedom from my inability to communicate with words. I knew somewhere within me, something unrecognizable was happening – some inner strength – and it really felt good! I welcomed it! Bobby and Rita

saw me swaying to the music and when they clapped their hands, I would also. Their mouths opened wide and they said, "Dad, Mom, Collie can hear. Watch her as she claps and sways to the Christmas carols."

Chapter 2

A Move

Steve and Karen began to see that maybe I really could learn something. I hoped they would stop looking at my outward appearance and see me as I believe I am – a person who cannot speak or hear but is able to communicate in other ways; someone who has value and can give love and is desperate to receive love. Their plan was to send me to a school for the deaf in Indianapolis where we lived, but, then, Steve, my foster father, lost his job. For the next year and a half, Steve tried to find work with no success, as no one could give him the income necessary to keep his family secure. He then heard other cities were hiring, and jobs he was qualified for were available in a city northeast of Indianapolis, called Fort Wayne, Indiana. He found a job in Fort Wayne making automobile axels, so we moved north. The wages and benefits were good, so Steve and Karen were happy again and we would be well provided for.

Bobby was 20 years old, so he decided to remain in Indianapolis with some friends he had grown up with. Rita was too young to be on her own, and she was no longer concerned about having to share Steve and Karen's attention with Bobby and me. Rita was finally seeing herself as an only child and enjoying all of the attention.

Steve and Karen enrolled me in a sign language class at a college called Indiana-Purdue at Fort Wayne. This decision turned out to be one of the best things that ever happened to me. Mostly deaf people joined the class, although speaking people wanting to learn signing for their deaf children, or wanting to communicate with deaf people at work or at church, liked the class. It opened up wonderful friendships for me. I finally was given the opportunity and ability outside of my family to be accepted. I felt real, genuine love for the first time.

Chapter 3

Gaining Confidence

My signing instructor's name was Pam Parker. She was partially deaf and wore hearing aids in both ears. Pam was married and had two children. Her husband and children had excellent hearing. She taught all of them to sign fluently. Consequently, they were able to sign and communicate with her and her friends.

Pam encouraged me to have my adopted parents take me somewhere once again to see if I would benefit from hearing aids or possible surgery. Steve and Karen agreed and took me to an audiologist who, again, told them, "I am sorry, but Collie's condition was caused from a birth defect, most likely hereditary, and cannot be reversed."

Sometimes, when I thought about Steve and Karen and doubted their love for me they would surprise me with doctor's appointments to help me. I then realized they did love me in their own way, but just didn't express it with hugs and physical contact, like a kiss on the cheek or a squeeze so I would not feel so alone.

In class one day Pam signed to me, as she formed the words for lip reading, "Collie, you are a very quick, astute learner. If you practice each and every day between your classes, you could be able to sign more words and sentences in a very short time. You need to sign with other deaf signers, so you can do it fluently."

Pam's enthusiasm was so contagious that I practiced night and day. When I couldn't sign with friends, I would practice in front of a mirror. Signing with my deaf friends could be used in so many different ways; it gave me the courage and hope to maybe find a job.

My friend, Christine Scott, was deaf and belonged to a theater group. I watched her interact with deaf and hearing people. She was not afraid to attempt anything despite her handicap. She danced to the music on stage as much as I had danced to the Christmas carols played on the piano years before. Vibration from music was her answer to stage performance.

There were several deaf plays being performed at a local theater in downtown Fort Wayne. Christine was almost always the featured star. Besides being talented, she was also very pretty, with brilliant red hair. The color reminded me of the Cardinal birds popular in Indiana. They are also called the Indiana Red Bird and are our official state bird. Christine's eyes are blue and she is approximately five feet, seven inches tall. She is quite lean and displays a great deal of poise and grace.

I signed to her, "What gives you the confidence to do these things despite your handicap?"

Christine replied, "Signing. I was born deaf like you, Collie. However, I was not abandoned. My parents gave me so many advantages, among them signing and the richness of total love and support. Along with learning to communicate, I began to attend My Savior Christian Church every Sunday. My pastor's name is Thomas Shelling. He speaks to all of us about Jesus Christ and that Jesus is the Son of God. He told us God so loved the world that He gave His only begotten Son to die for us, so that we may have eternal life. I then realized, Collie, that if God loved the world so much, He loves me just as well, because I live in His world. This is what gives me confidence: God's Son, Jesus Christ, lives in me and I live in Him! I know this doesn't make much sense to you, Collie, right now, but give it some thought. God loves you just as much as He loves me." She concluded her conversation with, "If you would like to come with me to church, I would like to bring you."

Weeks later I thought about attending church with Christine, yet I was inwardly troubled. She was never abandoned and her parents showed her a lot of love and support, so how could she possibly understand me and my living as an adopted child with virtual strangers as parents and siblings? She could never understand the lack of being loved and touched. There is a powerful difference between our upbringings.

Christine and I became inseparable, with the exception of my not attending church. We went to movies and especially loved comedies, the *Little Rascals* being one of our favorites. We could read lips fluently. We would clap our hands as many times as we desired. We could not hear the clapping, but we knew how to express ourselves when we liked something. We must have expressed our love for the movies a lot, because we were kicked out for annoying others! We clapped at the wrong times and sometimes made gurgling noises. We didn't care, nor were we aware, we bothered others. We were just having fun! We could not stop laughing no matter how hard we tried, and continued to mimic in our annoying way.

After we were kicked out of the theater, Christine signed, "That's okay, Collie. That manager will be sorry he kicked us out! Someday, I will be back here starring in a movie he will be showing. Then he will give us star attention and I will have you right beside me. You can be my agent or something."

We both laughed harder. There was no doubt in my mind she would be back revealing her many talents in that particular movie theater. Christine had so much finesse and talent and was perfectly aware of her abilities. Just being with her elevated my confidence. I began to finally believe in myself!

Chapter 4

Independence

I was now past 18. I wanted to be independent of Steve and Karen, and Rita as well, and made many attempts to find a job. I also knew I would need to find an apartment. I was beginning to get a nervous stomach and more frightened as I began my search. True to my fears, as I began the process of applying at a few places, I was rejected and turned down because of my inability to speak, poor vision, and deafness. I did have 20/20 vision in my left eye and knew if somebody would just give me a chance, since I had learned to compensate with my handicaps, I would do well.

After searching for weeks, I applied at the local library. My handicap did not threaten them in the least and they hired me. I was so happy! I cleaned shelves and sorted books after identifying the authors. I categorized them, placing them within easy access of the readers. I was unable to work the front, check-out desk due to my inability to speak, among other handicaps, but I loved my job and felt very useful!

I enjoyed reading autobiographies and fiction. Actually, I enjoyed everything I could get my hands on. I noticed that many deaf people came to the library, and I enjoyed helping them and using my signing skills. My working hours were excellent: 8:00 a.m. until 4:00 p.m., six days a week. Some evenings I stayed until 8:00. I never grew weary of my job and felt I found my niche in life.

I began a three-week search for an apartment and finally located a small one downtown, close to the library. It was a lower-level apartment with a small living room, one bedroom/bath, and a small kitchen. It was very suitable for my needs. A grocery store, restaurant, and a beautiful park set in the woods with numerous pathways and flowers were at my doorstep. Butterflies, birds, and small varmints came close to me when I walked home. I always wished I could speak to them and hear them speak to me in their special languages.

My adopted parents, Steve and Karen, were excited and extremely pleased for me. Rita also was pleased in that she was now the only child...and how she loved it! Steve and Karen helped me move and gave me a chair, end tables, lamps, and a couch. Steve even gave me his favorite ottoman! They also gave me the same bed I had when I lived with them, along with the dresser. Karen gave me her old pots and pans and extra dishes and linens. I was what they signed to me "ready to begin housekeeping." My very own place and free to be my own person! Now that I look back at Steve and Karen, I know they loved me. They just were not the hugging/kissing kind.

Once I began to get settled in I purchased a few items: flowers, paintings, and household decorations. The majority of my salary was used for rent, utilities, groceries, and an occasional movie or treat. Closed-caption television was approved in 1976 and would begin in 1980. It was almost 1980 now, so I bought a small black-and-white television with a decoder. I watched the *Ed Sullivan Show, Barney Miller,* and movies of all kinds. I especially loved *Barney Miller*! Sometimes my hours at work would change and I was required to stay longer in the evenings. I missed some of my favorite TV shows, three of them actually, and then would remember how fortunate and happy I was to have a job I loved.

I have lived in silence my whole life, so reading and being alone in my room was not uncomfortable. However, I still longed for companionship, hugs, kisses, and security. I hoped to find someone someday, but I was only 21 so it wasn't a great concern.

Chapter 5

The Attack

As I neared my 23rd birthday, I hoped Christine would come home to spend it with me. My friends signed to me that they have been reading reviews in magazines and newspapers regarding her theatre group. She is traveling in various states, performing in large and small towns, so it is not likely she will make it home. I miss her so much and am anxious for her return.

I met a girl at the library, Jeanna Babcock. She is 21 years old and we have become good friends. She is not deaf, but I taught her how to sign and to read my signs. She is a quick study and, after a few months, has become very proficient at lip reading, so we communicate very well. Jeanna was in an automobile accident when she was a young teenager. Her father was driving when a drunk driver pulled out in front of them. Her mother was killed and Jeanna's leg was broken in many places. She now and forever will walk with a limp. However, she feels fortunate she and her father survived. We laugh at what a pair we are together. Sometimes going through the park to my apartment, walking side by side, my bad eye is on her bad-leg side and I bump into her, nearly knocking her over. She stumbles, grabs my arms, and laughs, and I clap my hands, yell out noises, and sometimes gurgle. She is never offended by my gurgling or noise making. I knew we were good friends! She works as a dispatcher for the Fort Wayne Police Department and lives in an apartment close to her job, which is only six blocks away from mine.

Jeanna met and was attracted to a young police officer, Kevin Appleman. He is so handsome and totally dedicated to Jeanna. He is generous and kind and it is obvious he loves her. She was worried she was getting serious with him and afraid of his getting injured on the job. I signed to her, "Too late. Not to worry, you are already in love and serious with him!"

On Friday night, June 8, I worked late. After work, I took a shortcut through the park because I wanted to watch the *Little Rascals* again now that I had closed-caption TV and find it more enjoyable. Suddenly, I was grabbed from behind and dragged off the pathway, down a hill, and deep into the woods. I thought I was going to die. I could not hear anything, nor could I scream. I was knocked to the ground, but I attempted to fight back. I slapped at the man and fought him, kicking and screaming with my strange noises. However, he was much too strong and hit me in the face. I blacked out. When I regained consciousness and became aware of my surroundings, he was gone. He did not steal my purse or money, but left me without my virginity or my dignity.

Fortunately, a young couple walking through the park found some of my books in the pathway and some I had held onto, along with my purse. All were scattered down the hillside into the woods. They later told the police they could hear strange screeching sounds like an injured animal coming from within the woods and almost decided not to check any further but saw my purse and shoe. So they ran to the nearest telephone and called the police. When Jeanna received the call, she dispatched the police to the park. She felt certain the woman was me, because she knew I had cut through the park many times when I worked late. Jeanna could barely stand it until she knew who had been attacked. Two officers arrived. One was Kevin and Jeanna was with them. They took me to the nearest hospital for an examination to confirm the molestation and beating.

Chapter 6

The Aftermath

I signed that I really didn't know what my attacker looked like, but his breath was rancid and he was sweating profusely. His smell was horrendous. I sobbed and flailed my arms uncontrollably until the doctor gave me a shot to help me relax. I signed to Jeanna, "Why me, Jeanna? I have dark, straight hair, one brown eye and the other eye is lifeless, without defining color, glazed from blindness. I am ugly!"

The doctor and nurse explained to Jeanna that it was an act of violence, not attraction. I didn't feel any better about the whole crime and spent a sedated night in the hospital. The next day, Kevin and Jeanna took me home. I signed to Jeanna, "What if he knows where I live?"

Kevin searched my house to make sure it was safe and to give me comfort. He said it was okay for me to remain there. Jeanna offered to stay with me, but I declined, as I wanted to be alone.

After they left, I locked the apartment door. I was thankful it was the weekend and had two days off work to be alone and gather my thoughts. I knew the wounds inside me would never heal! I didn't want Steve and Karen to know what happened, as I wasn't sure of their reaction. I hadn't seen them for nearly a year and didn't want them hovering over me and feeling sorry for me, which I wasn't sure they even would.

I had a wonderful neighbor, an older woman named Sarah. We wrote notes to communicate. She telephoned the library on Monday to report I was ill and would need the week off. I was happy I had vacation time built up. The week off gave me time to cry a lot and think about what I was going through, and had been through. I also wondered how I was going to deal with it. I was thankful to be alive but sure the rest of my life would be filled with the fear of men. Even worse, I would be afraid to enter my beloved park!

I returned to work the following Monday and went into the office of the head librarian. I explained to her the entire episode and she informed the rest of the staff. The whole staff was very supportive and many offered to drive me home for the next several weeks. I accepted their rides and wondered if I would ever walk in the park again.

Kevin asked me to come down to the station and look at mug shots of the assailant. I signed to Jeanna that I never got a look at his face, so I couldn't identify him.

Jeanna signed, "Did he wear any rings or jewelry?"

I signed that I didn't see anything like that before I blacked out. My thoughts before I gave into blackness were "Christine, where is your God now? You said He loves me."

About six months later, another young woman was attacked and raped in the same park near my apartment. This woman recognized the assailant from mug shots, so he was arrested and jailed. Kevin and Jeanna came to tell me the man had confessed to attacking me and three other women in the past six months. They did not need my identity testimony, because I never saw his face. I did feel safer after he was convicted and sent to prison. Slowly, my life began to resemble and return to what it had been before this most traumatic and intimate incident happened.

I was at work several months later, placing books on shelves, when I turned around and saw Christine smiling at me. I dropped the books, clapped my hands together, and began crying. She grabbed me. We laughed, hugged, and jumped up and down. I was so happy to see her!

Sharon Kurtz Hammel

When I got off work, she was waiting for me. We walked to the small restaurant near my apartment. Our hands were flying a mile a minute as we signed, trying to make up for lost time. Finally, we calmed down and Christine signed, "I am still traveling with the Fort Wayne theater group."

Chapter 7

God Has a Plan and Purpose

"I am enjoying the different cities and sites. Doors have opened for me and I am getting well known on the West Coast," Christine said.

I signed, "Christine, I am so happy for you."

When I told her what I had been through and how I had survived molestation and being beaten, she cried with me. She then took both of my hands, looked into my eyes, and began to sign, "Collie, God spared your life. He has a purpose and a plan for you. Do not let what happened make you bitter or not want to know and trust God. Do not distrust all men! Somewhere out there in this big world is a man God has already chosen for you. Please believe me on this, because I know God loves you and has a purpose for you."

Once again, I wanted to believe her, but I never experienced God's love, or love from anyone, with the exception of other deaf people who understood where I was coming from. I changed the subject and told her I was proud of her achievements.

She shared stories of the theater, the cast, their love affairs, and the fun times when they traveled. In fact, she was leaving the next day for Reno, Nevada. She and some of her fellow cast members were going to a cabin to relax and ski.

Christine met a man while on tour who she really enjoyed being with; however, she wanted to pursue her career and not get serious. They had been seeing one another for a couple of years. He would be flying into Reno the next day from his home in Gig Harbor, Washington. I was extremely happy for her and did not feel envious at all! But I did wonder if I would ever meet someone or even want to after all I had been through.

Christine left to pursue her career and I resumed my normal routine, putting behind me the trauma I had endured.

My job at the library began a class in sign language for anyone who had an interest in learning. The staff asked me to lead the class. I realized I would need a person who could speak to them as well as sign to them. I asked Jeanna, but she had filled her life with her job and she and Kevin were extremely busy.

A few months earlier, I met another woman who had the ability to speak and sign. Her name is Glenna Sutton. She is in her thirties, married, and has a deaf son, Jeff, who is 15. She had a great deal of experience in signing over the years and she and Jeff were willing to work with me and the students.

The class was a 12-week course, and we had seven students to start. Eventually, we reduced the size to five, as two of the students felt it was not the class for them. They could already speak and hear pretty well; therefore, they said it was too difficult for them to learn to sign. My life was filled with work, teaching, and making new friends.

On my 25th birthday, Jeanna and Kevin invited me on a blind date to celebrate my day. I was so nervous, because I had never dated anyone before and was not sure what to do. I certainly could not talk to the man!

Jeanna signed to me, "Collie, Jerry is deaf, also. You have a lot in common and will enjoy his company. Kevin is even beginning to sign and is happy to be learning. He will use the sign in his work from time to time, as police officers often run into situations where signing is used. I encouraged him to sign and he is doing very well."

The four of us went to dinner and had a wonderful time! Jerry and I signed and lip read and Kevin and Jeanna joined in with us. We signed that we would be getting together again soon, but I never heard from

Jerry. My thought was what is wrong with me? In my opinion, I am as normal as Jerry.

Jeanna signed, "Collie, like you, he has never dated before. I think he was afraid or just not yet ready. I believed you and him to be a good match!"

Again, it was just not meant to be!

Chapter 8

Meeting Isaiah

February 1984. I turned 27 years old. I felt as though the years were slipping away and my life was going nowhere.

I received a letter from Christine. She wrote that she was starring in many theaters throughout the West Coast. She was enjoying all the many plays and movies she was in and becoming famous. I always predicted she would be famous and a big star someday. All of her previous letters over the years reinforced that belief.

My job was still interesting and I enjoyed signing with the help of my deaf and speaking friends. I seemed to be doing more teaching now, yet I still enjoyed the library work as well. Despite the busy workload, my life was lonely. I looked forward to meeting someone who I believed would enhance my life and give me hope and something to look forward to.

Late one afternoon, after my sign class, Donna, my supervisor, came to me and signed, "Collie, there is a young man who will be joining your class. His name is Isaiah Miller. He began to lose his hearing at a young age, and it is getting worse. He wants to learn sign language before his hearing is totally gone."

Upon our introduction, I felt like someone had kicked me in the stomach! I felt nervous, happy, excited, and sick to my stomach all at the same time. When he shook my hand, his palm was sweaty and his hand was shaking as hard as mine. Right away I knew this is a man who will be important to me. His smile made my heart jump, though his style of dress was unusual. I noticed his coat had no buttons or button holes. He had on a broad-brimmed hat with black felt around it. When he removed his hat, I noticed his hair was blunt cut and had bangs in front like a girl would wear. He had on black shoes and his pants were held up by suspenders. Even though we were unable to communicate, I noticed his keen interest in the sign language alphabet display around the library.

Donna explained to him that I would begin by teaching the alphabet first. He nodded at me and took a chair next to Glenna's son, Jeff. By this time, Jeff was well advanced in signing and had been helping me with classes for five years. Being a fluent lip reader, I observed Jeff and Isaiah and knew he would quickly learn this new language. Having spent several weeks with Isaiah, we were able to exchange many signs; and with lip reading, he progressed more rapidly than I had even anticipated.

In sign, he said to me, "Collie, I am of the Old Order Amish and Mennonite people. Have you ever been around my kind of people before?"

I signed, "No, but I am interested in knowing more about you and your people. If your dress is any indication of how your people differ from me, then I want to know more."

Isaiah signed in response, "Maybe someday I can take you to my home and have you meet my family. Our dress and customs are definitely different than yours! We are generally unaccustomed to inviting strangers into our homes; however, you are different, as you are my teacher and will be accepted as such!"

I signed in return, "I have many questions about your customs. For example, how your women dress, some of your problems, your education, what your weddings are like, etc. You signed that Mennonites are different and I would like to know how they are different. I would really like to learn your ways and try to understand the differences. Then, again, my world is vastly different than most people! I am delighted and happy to have you as part of our class and pleased you are learning my language so well. Do you have many deaf people in the Amish community?"

"We have some children who are deaf," Isaiah signed in return, "and the elderly are losing their hearing. In my immediate family, I am the only person losing my hearing at such a young age. I do, however, have two cousins who are deaf. I plan to learn all I can and teach them what you are teaching me."

After class, Isaiah gave me a note saying, "I will try and arrange for someone to bring me to the library for the next sign class. Another one of our customs is our mode of travel. It is by horse and buggy, not automobile. We are, however, allowed to ride as a passenger with someone who owns an automobile. We are just not able to own them! This is another of our older Amish beliefs."

I signed, "I do not understand that concept. I have never been able to drive due to my handicaps; however, many of my friends take me with them when they want to go places. I cannot fathom the concept of not being allowed to drive, when one is fully capable of driving."

"Once again, this is our belief, and many of our beliefs will appear strange to you!"

Chapter 9

The Invitation

Before I knew it, almost a year had gone by. Isaiah had become fluent in sign and taught his cousins and others in his community how to get by communicating with the hearing people in his family and town. He no longer needed my assistance. I was happy he and I had developed a friendship.

Early one evening, my signal light flashed in the living room, indicating there was someone at the door. Isaiah was standing there smiling at me. His friend, Bill, had an automobile and brought him. He was the same man who brought him back and forth to classes. He asked me if I would like to come to his home and meet his family on Saturday. Since I no longer work on Saturdays I readily agreed. Bill has to pick up medical prescription drugs on Saturday anyway, so he will pick me up and take me back with them. My whole week was a blur. I eagerly awaited a change in my normal routine.

I was unsure how to dress appropriately. I knew nothing about what the Amish would consider acceptable. After trying on many outfits Saturday morning, I selected a plain, calf-length dress. Apparently it was a good choice, because Isaiah smiled and nodded at me when I opened the door.

I was overwhelmed at the scenery and mode of travel as we approached Isaiah's home. I saw so many horse and buggies on the road with automobiles and trucks. The homes had unbelievable arrays of flowers and small gardens. Everything looked so clean.

White picket fences surrounded the homes and laundry hung out on clothes lines.

One home we passed had laundry hanging from the front porch of the house with two pulley attachments that went to the top portion of a large barn window with another pulley. The laundry hung the length of the yard. All the women had to do was hang the clothes on the rope and use the pulley to bring the clothes back around to the house.

They would reload it with more laundry and go back to the barn with the pulley, then back again to the house. It was a fascinating process to watch!

I wanted to ride around all day looking at each farm house. There were so many goats, cows, horses, sheep, dogs, cats, and chickens. I saw so many beautiful children running around barefoot. The girls wore plain, brown, green, or blue dresses, almost to their ankles. They had cap-type head coverings. Their little cheeks were rosy red and very healthy looking. They, along with the boys, were laughing.

The boys looked like the men in their black pants with suspenders and plain shirts. They wore straw hats with black ribbon around them. They also were barefoot. What a memorable trip this was going to be! This is Isaiah's world and it is wonderful.

We approached a small town called Topeka, Indiana. Almost every person was in Amish dress. I looked at Isaiah. He was smiling at me. He signed, "Collie, you look like a child who is seeing the world for the first time." I let him know in sign that I believed this to be the most exciting day for me and one I will always remember. Living first in Indianapolis and then Fort Wayne was so different from this life. I wanted to absorb each moment and relish this gift of simplicity.

Soon we arrived in another town called Shipshewana, Indiana. It was not large, yet bigger than Topeka. It had many more shops and also many more people. Isaiah signed that the people were buying seeds to plant. We turned into a driveway that approached Isaiah's family home. Two small children ran out onto the steps to see us. I glanced around and saw a big red barn. Three boys were coming out of the barn door. There were white fences surrounding the yard and again so many beautiful flowers.

An older man appeared from the back of the house. He had a beard and wore a straw hat with a black band around it. His face was weather beaten from the sun. He had the kindest blue eyes I had ever seen. Isaiah introduced me as his teacher from Fort Wayne. "My father has expressed his pleasure in meeting you. He wants you to feel welcome here."

Signing to Isaiah, I said, "Tell your father I am honored to meet him and thank you for having me in your home."

Isaiah's mother came out of the house by a side door. She wore a plain, dark blue dress. Her hair was pulled back in a bun resting at the back of her head with a white small head covering. She wore black stockings and shoes. Her smile lit up her face like the sun and her green eyes gave the same warmth. Isaiah signed, "My mother welcomes you, Collie. Her name is Rebekah." I observed that Isaiah and the children signed that they all call her "Mem."

His mother insisted they call me by my given name, Colette. Isaiah signed, "That is our custom, to use our God-given names. You saw some of my brothers when we arrived. Amos is 17, Jacob is 15, and Joseph is 14. My sisters are Deborah 12, Ruth 10, and Leah 8."

Isaiah and I walked around the yard. He showed me the barn that housed the horses. We also walked around the flower beds similar to the ones I enjoyed seeing on the trip. A large vegetable garden to the east of the house was arranged in the center, with

flowers all around the outside edges. Everything was so orderly, clean, and neat. Isaiah signed, "Each person living here has a job to do. We have many chores and all work together to make a living for our family. During your stay this weekend, you will observe us doing our daily chores, and this will give you a glimpse into our daily lives. I hope you will enjoy your stay."

It was already early evening and I signed to Isaiah, "While you are doing chores, may I help your mother in the kitchen? Will you ask her?"

Rebekah was very pleased and showed me what she did to prepare the meal for her family. I reached into my bag to bring out my tablet and pencil so we could communicate. With the girls ranging from eight to 12 years old, they were quite capable of doing a lot of work, so I observed them. I was fascinated with all of the food they prepared!

Chapter 10

Lifestyle Differences

There was not one electrical appliance in the Miller home. Rebekah used an old cook stove and many hands. We had fried chicken, coleslaw, molded salad, homemade bread, sliced tomatoes, homemade pies, fresh milk, and coffee. Isaiah later signed to me, "Amish people of this community eat from the land. If the garden is beautiful, so is one's table!"

I was impressed with the prayer given by Joshua prior to the meal. I was unaccustomed to praying before a meal, at bedtime, or, for that matter, anytime! Joshua thanked God for the blessings upon their land and he praised Him for His provisions and the skills to use their hands for the abundance they have, to be shared with others. The prayer of thanksgiving was entirely new for me. I was glad Isaiah signed the prayer his father gave from his heart.

Later, Isaiah and I walked and talked. He signed, "Collie, our Amish culture has a simple piety, a desire to be faithful to God." He went on to say that you will not find choirs, robes, altars, organs, and pews in their church. You won't see professional pastors or stained-glass windows, either, like you see in Fort Wayne.

"Our faith believes the Bible is God's Word and that Jesus is the Son of God, who died for our salvation because of our sins. We focus on a daily practice of this belief, rather than worshipping in a sanctuary on Sunday."

"Isaiah, Christine invited me to her church. She told me some of what you are saying, except she worships in the church sanctuary."

Isaiah signed in response, "When the demands of Church and State differ, the Amish seek to follow the Word of God, even if it means humiliation or imprisonment. The Amish believe religious faith should be practiced, not displayed, and translated into daily living. I hope, as you spend time with us, you will understand our love for Jesus."

We returned to a house lit up by kerosene lanterns. Once again, I observed no electricity. Some candles were also placed throughout the room. I was amazed there were no light switches to turn on and off!

That evening, as was their custom, Joshua read the Bible and all of Isaiah's family sat and listened. Isaiah signed to me the 23rd Psalm and I felt a new surge of love within me! Soon it was time to go to bed, as everyone gets up early for church.

Rebekah showed me to a bedroom, which I believe Ruth and Leah doubled up in order to provide for me. I noticed a beautiful quilt lying on top of the bed and she wrote on my tablet, "Deborah, Ruth, and Leah made this." It was so comfortable, even though it was hot outside. I wanted to feel the quality of their work covering me when I lied down. I looked out the window and noticed there were no curtains or blinds. The moon and stars shone so brightly that no lantern or lighting of any kind was needed. I slept as I had never slept before, peaceful and feeling totally accepted.

On Sunday morning, I awoke to a delicious food smell and was treated to a breakfast of fresh fruit, bacon, eggs, biscuits and homemade gravy, coffee, and fresh milk. Isaiah signed to me, "Collie, we do our own butchering and meat preparation, we smoke and cure our hams, bacon, and bologna. You have seen our garden grow wonderful, fresh vegetables. We also raise our own chickens and fish from a stream nearby. Mem, Deborah, Ruth, and Leah can bushels of fruit each summer. Many Amish have their own fruit trees and make their own applesauce. They also shell their own peas and harvest their own beans.

A great deal of time and energy is devoted to our eating well. We feel we do not need a big budget, if we use the gifts God has given us!"

After breakfast was served and the chores were done, everyone moved quickly to get ready for church. When we arrived at church, Isaiah signed, "The songs are sung in German." I don't understand German, so Isaiah signed them to me in English.

There were no instruments, which was okay with me, as I couldn't hear them anyway! Isaiah signed that the ancient tunes are sung from memory and the leaders decide which member will preach at a private meeting at the beginning of the service, during the opening hymn by the congregation. An opening sermon will normally last 30 minutes, followed by the main sermon, which can last up to three hours.

The church was a couple of miles from Isaiah's home and they had some benches set up in a barn. Even though the church was completely new to me, and hard to follow, I enjoyed the simplicity of the message of hope, faith, community giving, and yielding to God's will because of God's Son, Jesus Christ, who died for our sins. The simplicity of the church being at one of the family's or friend's home made it more special.

Isaiah signed, "The practice of living in a simple manner and helping our neighbors in need is of utmost importance to us. The hearts of each individual and the gathering of Christians are the sacred ingredients of worship. Therefore, crosses and complicated rituals are not required or needed. When the worship service ends, a common meal will be prepared by the women. It will be served at noon. This practice is accomplished 26 times a year at each other's homes, or every other Sunday throughout the year."

Chapter 11

A Reminder

After Sunday services and the meal, we traveled back to Isaiah's home, where his friend, Bill, arrived to take me back to Fort Wayne. I had a glorious weekend and stepped completely out of my comfort zone! I witnessed a humble lifestyle that I loved and already knew I wanted to be a part of someday – hopefully on a permanent basis, even if it didn't include Isaiah.

I sat down and wrote Christine a letter and shared with her about my wonderful weekend. I told her I had received an insight into her God and His Son, Jesus Christ. I told her I wanted to learn more about Him and was happy she shared her love for Jesus with me before I met Isaiah.

Upon returning to work, my routine seemed dull and boring for the next couple of weeks. I did enjoy teaching my sign classes again and soon became absorbed in my old way of life. I didn't hear from Isaiah for months, but understood that his busy way of life left him little time to visit or correspond. His time was devoted to working the fields and growing crops. A farmer's work is never done!

Summer was coming to an end when Jeanna and Kevin announced their upcoming marriage. I was so pleased and happy for them! September 17 was the date they chose and she asked me to be her bridesmaid. She had already purchased her wedding dress. We shopped together for just the right clothes for me. She told me she wanted me to feel beautiful for her day!

When the wedding day approached, we were both excited, and Kevin was ever so happy. The church was decorated with pale, lilac colors and scented, pale-yellow roses, Jeanna's favorite flowers. It was a pretty wedding and I was extremely proud to be a part of it. She was simply beautiful and Kevin was very proud and obviously very much in love. They decided to remain in Fort Wayne, as his job was still with the police force, and she would continue as a dispatcher.

Later in September, after the wedding, Isaiah came to the library to see me. He wanted to know if I would be interested in moving to Shipshewana on a permanent basis, to teach sign language classes to his deaf friends and relatives. He said there were still some deaf children who needed to learn.

He signed, "Collie, I would be so pleased if you would come. The elders met with me and we will pay you. You can live with our family and I will help you get started until we can make other arrangements. Please say yes, we need and want you! The children have been practicing the 'I Love You' sign you taught them. They run around the yard with their thumb, forefinger, and little finger sticking up. It's quite a sight to see! You will also find that children will help each other with signing."

"Isaiah, your culture is vastly different from mine. Your schools are different, as well."

"Yes they are! The Amish are not opposed to education; we are just against education higher than our needs – education we do not need. A practical, down-to-earth, elementary education is good enough to prepare us for success in our culture. An eighth-grade education anchored in reading, writing, and arithmetic is enough for our life. In the early 1950s, our church leaders decided to operate their own one-room schools. Students attended one-room schools through the eighth grade. We were told that state law required attendance until the age of 15, meaning one year in public high school. Amish leaders and public officials met and agreed to compromise. We devised an Amish vocational program, where 14-year-olds were required to attend a weekly vocational school in an Amish home after completing eighth grade. For three hours a week, an Amish teacher instructs a dozen or so youth in practical vocational skills, business, math, reading, and writing. Students will keep a weekly diary of their work, which the teacher will look over. In 1972, the U.S. Supreme Court gave its legal blessing to the Amish schools. Today, Amish children attend one-room Amish elementary schools. Typically, the teachers are single Amish women."

I signed in return, "I like to watch *Little House on the Prairie* and what you are saying reminds me of that show."

"What you are saying makes no sense to me. We are not allowed to watch television, if that is to what you are referring. Nor do we have electricity, as you noted on your recent visit. If you teach signing to our children, it will help our people keep pace with modern ways, without jeopardizing our traditional values. Please think about it."

"I will consider it and will let you know soon. If I do this, I will need to give notice to the library and complete the class I am teaching now. I have one month left to complete this teaching session and be finished."

After Isaiah left, and for the remainder of the week, I thought of nothing else! I even picked up the *King James Version* of the Holy Bible that Jeanna and Kevin gave me for being their bridesmaid. I began reading it and praying God would provide an answer.

I began relying on God more and more every day. By the end of the week, I had my answer: I would move to Shipshewana.

"Dear Christine, I am sending this note to tell you I will be moving to Shipshewana, Indiana. This is a big step for me, as I have only lived in two places and will no longer have my Fort Wayne friends around me, especially you! I will be totally dependent on Isaiah's family and will be teaching full-time. My concerns are legitimate, yet my eagerness to live and thrive in the Amish world is greater than my concerns. Please be happy for me. When I am settled in my new life, I will send you my new address."

I mailed the letter the next day and was excited to begin my new journey and start a new life.

Chapter 12

A New Life

The library staff was very pleased for me, because they knew how much I enjoyed teaching. This new adventure would be good for me! They also expressed their sorrow to see me leave. Many of the deaf students I had taught came to say goodbye, and we had coffee, cake, cookies, and punch. At last I was ready to say goodbye to my old way of life and hello to a new life.

Isaiah and his driver friend, Bill, picked me up and we began my second journey to Shipshewana and Amish country. It was the early part of October and the trees were so colorful and much different than when I had been there in late spring. After living in the city for so long, once again I was amazed at the country beauty.

The horses and buggies traveling at five miles per hour were no match for the automobiles and large trucks traveling 60 miles per hour, but Bill was a good driver and watchful of the cars and trucks as he approached cresting hills and sharp corners. Isaiah signed to me, "Collie, high-beam headlights and honking horns can startle horses into dangerous behavior. We pray that automobile and truck drivers are careful and watching the road ahead of them. When you see horses at a hitching rail or harnessed to a buggy, please don't feed them. People startle them with attention and, again, dangerous things can happen."

I signed in return, "I will be cautious when I approach the horses, thank you for informing me." I then noticed how fast cars and trucks were going when they came up behind the buggies.

"Are there a lot of accidents on these roads with the horses and buggies?" I asked.

"Yes, there a lot of them," he answered. "People always seem to be in a hurry! Sometimes we are criticized for going too slow; however, it is the car/truck that kills, not the horse and buggy!"

I thought about his answer and realized I would never be able to drive a car or do anything but ride in a buggy, because I could not hear horns honking or cars approaching and passing. I was worried about Isaiah after his hearing was gone. I wondered if he would accept it and be able to manage. Soon, we were in Isaiah's home with his family.

Isaiah signed to me, "Collie, in the days to come, you are going to meet with the Bishop, who is responsible for our Church Settlement District, meaning the District in which we currently live. There are many Districts. You will be interviewed by the Bishop and many others. Upon completion of the interview process, you will be accepted as a teacher for the deaf children. My father and I have spoken to all of the people who will interview you. We have never had a deaf teacher, so the rules will be different than our other Amish teachers, because you are unique in the way you teach. Does this meet with your approval?"

"Yes, it does, and thanks to you and your father, Isaiah."

"Collie, you are under no obligation to stay here and teach. You can decide at any time if this is not for you and can return to Fort Wayne."

"I like the challenge and thank you for giving me this opportunity. I look forward to the interview process and finding out about all of the expectations required of me."

That evening, prior to retiring and at the end of Joshua's Bible reading, I signed to Isaiah, "Will you ask your family to pray for me to have a successful interview?"

The following morning, after breakfast, Isaiah took me around the countryside once again. Previously when I was here, I had only been on major roads and the entrance to his home. Despite the fall temperatures, with a sharp wind indicative of the weather to come, I enjoyed the country roads and scenery. The horse and buggy were somewhat sheltered from the wind and I could see what seemed like miles of country farmland.

Isaiah signed to me, "Collie, since the Old Order Amish farm is a place to live and raise one's family, we're concerned, because, since this is the mid-1980s, almost all of our farmland has already been purchased. And we want to have plenty of land for our children to grow up and remain near us.

"Many of our young men are going to work in factories, not because of disbelief in our way of life, but for economic survival. One of the first factories Amish men worked for was Starcraft Corporation located in Topeka – the little town we came through to get here. Do you remember it?"

"Yes," I answered.

Isaiah continued, "Initially, they specialized in agriculture equipment. Then they became a galvanized steel boat factory for use in farm ponds. Later, they produced fiberglass boats and a variety of recreational vehicles. Many Amish men have worked in this plant, and this site was chosen because of the Amish and Mennonite work ethic. When the owner would need additional help, the Amish, known for their building skills, would be invaluable. The Amish are known for giving a day's work for a day's pay! It just seemed to happen that with farmland becoming scarcer, Amish men turned to factories. They would do their early morning chores then travel by horse and buggy to the factory. If the distance to the factory is quite long, groups of men will pay a driver to take them and pick them up when they are done. Generally they try to work closer or nearer to their homes.

"Their preference is to stay at home and work their fields of crops at their own pace, doing it right. An Amish prefers to be his own boss. The main reason is that conflict sometimes arises between employee and employer; and the Amish try to avoid conflict at any cost. If we are fortunate to work in a plant where the Amish way of life is respected, then it is not as bad. This environment allows us to be off for our special days: Good Friday, Ascension Day, and funerals, and this is a good working environment, as the plant manager is okay with it. The English who work there have weekends off for total rest and leisure. However, we continue to do our chores morning and evening and still work the whole week! When working away from the farm, we have less time with our families, which is most important in our lives. This has given you a lot to think about and I will return to this discussion and more about our Amish customs later."

As we continued to ride around the farmland area, I noticed a small building with several bicycles nearby. I signed to Isaiah, "What is that building over there?"

"That is one of our schools. It is a one-room school with a single teacher. The schoolhouse is chosen carefully for schooling, so there will be plenty of outdoor play area for children. They need a field large enough to play softball. Sometimes a skating pond for use during recess and lunch is also useful. The neighbors of the school have lanes they allow for sledding."

I signed, "I would never have believed this plain, simple school would exist anywhere."

I am so thrilled to have been asked to be a part of teaching these children! I cannot count how many times I thanked Isaiah for the privilege of being here. He nodded and smiled, almost embarrassed. Isaiah had evening chores to do and it was quickly approaching the middle of the afternoon. I enjoyed the country ride and learning more about his family and their customs. I welcomed this new way of life!

Chapter 13

Living off the Land

When I awoke in the morning to the sight of rain hitting the windows, I wished, once again, I could hear. I knew Joshua and Rebekah would be very thankful that their garden, hay, and pasture fields would receive a good boost.

After bathing from the bowl of hot water and dressing, I went downstairs. Deborah, Ruth, and Leah had breakfast on the table, which Rebekah had prepared. We had biscuits and sausage gravy, fried eggs, potatoes, cheese, juice, milk, and coffee. I signed to Isaiah, "I can't afford to eat this way every day or I will weigh 200 pounds!"

Isaiah said, "If you work hard, you will wear it off."

After breakfast, the girls began to wash dishes. While they were doing that, Rebekah began sewing their school dresses and making Joshua's pants.

I sat down with Rebekah and she began to teach me and allowed me to help her sew and mend. I finally began to feel useful! After the dishes were picked up and washed, the girls started to clean the main floor. We were so busy sewing and mending that, before I realized it, they started to prepare lunch from leftovers the night before. After lunch, dishes were washed again and the kitchen was cleaned. The girls then cleaned the bedrooms upstairs and the back porch. I continued to mend and Rebekah baked three rhubarb pies.

Amos, Jacob, and Joseph came in and Rebekah gave them all haircuts. It looked like she had placed a bowl on their heads and cut around it! The day was full of a variety of work, and each person knew their part and what was expected of them, just as Isaiah told me. After the haircuts, Rebekah had the girls hitch up their horse, Prince, to the buggy so they could go to the neighbors and pick up milk for the family.

Deborah and Ruth took one of Rebekah's homemade rhubarb pies to give to the neighbor. While they were gone, Rebekah began to cut material to make a dress for Deborah. I continued mending and wrote on my writing tablet, "Rebekah, may I watch and help you make pies the next time?" She gave me the same smile Isaiah gives me and nodded yes, obviously pleased with my request.

When we finished eating the evening meal and the girls washed the dishes, Joshua led everyone in prayer. He prayed for and gave thanks to God for the day's blessings. I was finally learning and growing accustomed to this ritual and enjoyed it. We all then cleaned up to retire for the night. It had been a busy and stimulating day for me and I was looking forward to the next day, and the next day after that! I was hoping to be interviewed soon for the teaching job.

The next few days were very busy, with each day being a learning process for all. I noticed the girls were picking up some signs between me and Isaiah. Rebekah got out rhubarb juice. What a treat that was! She wrote on my tablet that rhubarb had been plentiful in the spring last year. I told her I had never tasted rhubarb until she made the pies. I wrote, "It must be a fruit."

Rebekah wrote back that it is a vegetable but has many qualities of a fruit. It is very easy to grow and has been a mainstay of the Amish homemaker. It can be used to bake pies, breads, cakes, muffins, cookies, juices, and is even used in some soup recipes. She also wrote that over the winter months, she will have rhubarb every day. I looked forward to a new discovery, living with this special Amish family.

In the evening, after the chores were done and we had some free time, Isaiah and I walked around the land and he shared more stories about his culture. He signed, "By living in the country, farming is our life! One could not live in the city and be able to work the land without driving somewhere to do it! We consider farming the ideal occupation for Christians. We are not saying everyone should be farmers, only that it is an ideal way of life."

"In what way is it ideal?"

"In our daily contact with the land, we cannot help but stand in awe and wonder of God's creation. We can see His infinite wisdom; the cycle of life, death, and renewal. Our Father is having us all work together as a family. Not His work, or your work, or my work, but our work! The children grow up knowing how to work and accept responsibility."

"Thank you for that explanation, Isaiah. I see that played out every day I am here with your family."

We continued our walk and I signed, "May I have a lantern for my bedroom? On the weekends, I sometimes like to read at night. A candle will suffice if you do not have an extra lantern. Throughout the week, I am usually so tired I just fall into bed in the daylight." Isaiah gave me a lantern and showed me how to use it.

I brought my Bible with me and began to earnestly read. I thought over what Isaiah shared with me tonight about standing in awe of God's creation. I read in Genesis, the beginning of the Bible, specifically, that each day had an evening and a morning. This revealed to me once again that the days back then were the same as our days now. As I continued to read about creation, I knew I must accept the Bible's account of creation as accurate, along with everything I read from this point forward. Inwardly this was pleasing to me, and I knew I was gaining more knowledge of the Bible. My heart was beginning to accept it as well. I continued to see how God takes care of those who believe in Him, through His Son, Jesus Christ. I also witnessed this through the lives of Isaiah's family and friends. Psalm 37 spoke to me: "The meek shall inherit the earth and shall delight themselves in the abundance of peace."

The Amish do have such peace among themselves and with others. They acknowledge their dependence on the goodness and grace of God and display no arrogance toward their fellow man. The meekness of the people in this Amish community does influence others. Meekness, I have seen with my own eyes, is not a weakness but a gentleness of spirit that implies remarkable strength. As I continue to live with this family, it is only the beginning of a life I have wanted so badly – to be loved and accepted for who I am despite my handicaps. I will cherish each day I live here until God decides to move me or show me what direction my life will take next. But first I must learn to trust Him completely.

I went to sleep almost immediately after reflecting on the Scriptures I had read.

Chapter 14

The Dawdy Haus

The next morning when I awoke, the day was just breaking and I could smell breakfast cooking. I could also smell fresh coffee and noticed the quietness that comes with the men out doing their chores while Rebekah and the girls prepare food. This was all so refreshing to me!

As I walked down the stairs I could see through the window that it looked like a rain-free day. Maybe today Isaiah and I could take another tour of the land, or maybe this would be the day for my teaching interview. No matter what the day brought, I just knew it would be good. Once again, I experienced a wonderful peace within me I could not explain. It seemed to be happening to me more frequently. It must be a God thing!

After breakfast, Isaiah signed to me, "We will be taking another trip today and I will explain to you more about the Amish ways."

"I am looking forward to it!"

As we traveled the countryside, I saw more one-room schools. I signed to Isaiah, "You mentioned the Amish Districts to me before, how many are there? I'm guessing around 150 to 160." I wasn't really sure of those numbers, so he went on to explain.

"The older established settlements are perhaps that number but the newer settlements are smaller. You ask some interesting questions, Collie!"

"It is important for me to understand as much as I can about your way of life, and now my life here and how I will fit in."

We continued to ride through the countryside and I noticed cabinet and woodworking shops and harness and blacksmith shops. I made a mental note to ask Isaiah to take me to these shops while I am here, so I can watch the men perform their crafts. We did stop at the Miller Woodworking Shop. He wanted to show me the ability the Millers had in crafting various furniture pieces.

I was absorbed in watching their craft and talent when suddenly Isaiah signed to me to watch their conversation. I read their lips and was confused by the language they were using, as it didn't make sense to me.

"Collie, they and I are speaking in German, known here as Pennsylvania Dutch. It is important, as it is the language of sermons in church as well. You may not have noticed it before because the amount of people gathered together prevented you from reading their lips. I was signing to you in English and you didn't know the difference as you could not see them."

"I wish I could hear it spoken instead of signed!"

"English is used mainly with the non-Amish people, so, when you are present, you see my Mem, Daed, and siblings speaking to one another in English so you will be able to understand the lip reading. English is the instruction in Amish schools.

"The Old Order Amish continue to use German as we talk amongst ourselves. We enjoy using the language and pass it on to the children so it will never be forgotten. Pennsylvania Dutch and standard German are still used throughout our District and families."

"I can see how this tradition will always go on," I said, "knowing the number of Districts you told me are here in this area. I have also noticed some of the homes are larger and others look like they have added on rooms to them."

"You are correct," he signed. "The additions to the homes are being provided for our parents and grandparents as they age so they do not go into retirement facilities. If the family home is large enough they continue to live with everyone else; if not, then oftentimes an adjacent dwelling is provided where the grandparents take up residence. The added dwelling is called a Dawdy Haus. In this way, they are allowed to be involved with the family. The elderly parents are well respected and give important advice. They once helped raise the younger ones, therefore they are cared for in their old age in return. We often say in the Old Order Amish, 'We care for our people from cradle to grave.' Our lives can be confusing, as, once again, it differs from community to community and District to District.

"Amish lifestyle is dictated by the Ordung, which is German for order. Each church has its own set of rules to live by. Even in our own language, we can experience difficulty understanding others if we are out of our own geographical area."

The time was changing to midafternoon and it was getting somewhat chilly, so we decided to return to Isaiah's home. When we got back, Joshua told Isaiah that Josey Miller, the school board chairman, had stopped by to see him. They have an interview scheduled tomorrow for the teaching position. I was extremely excited, so I awoke very early the next morning.

Chapter 15

Approval

I could see the lighted lantern downstairs and knew Rebekah was up and the men were doing their chores. I dressed carefully to please the school board chairman, who would be conducting the interview this morning. When the school board chairman arrived, it was planned for him and Joshua to conduct the interview and Isaiah was to sign for me.

Mr. Josey Miller had a gentle manner and asked me questions about my sign experience and ability to teach others to sign. I signed that when I arrived in Fort Wayne I took sign classes at a college. The signs I use are a combination of signs that were taught to me. I explained that my deaf/hearing-impaired teacher was an excellent instructor who worked diligently to teach us correctly. With the ability to sign, I have received a gift I can pass on to help others. This is why I began to teach classes at the Fort Wayne library and where I became acquainted with Isaiah.

Then Josey Miller asked about my religious beliefs. I explained to him that I had not been a believer until a year ago. I explained that since I have been living with Joshua and his family, I have become a Bible reader. I attend worship services with the family. We pray together and God has revealed to me that His Son, Jesus Christ, is my Lord and

Savior. I am here to glorify God, to help fellow men, and prepare for the better life that is to come.

I explained that I am a new creature in God's Kingdom and need guidance, love, and patience as I continue to search for God. Joshua smiled and asked me what I would be teaching the children at prayer time.

"I will teach the finger spelling for the alphabet and to sign their names, then phrases. I will teach the practical skills of spelling, English, mathematics, geography and health. Lip reading will be very important as we learn to communicate more easily in sign. Later, they will come to learn the school lessons, but first the sign language.

"We will, then, learn to read the Bible and sign the words to each other. Whatever Scripture lesson we use for the day will be signed to one another. Besides all of that, we will be praying in sign. My language of sign will be different and confusing to them at first, but they will find a new world of understanding once they learn.

"I intend to use blackboards, charts, posters, and other visual aids to achieve their understanding. They are entering a world I have lived in all of my life. This is now a reality for them as well. I have developed a greater insight into the thoughts of those who are deaf. One seems to perceive a better and fuller understanding after losing one of the five senses. For example, the blind generally have sharper hearing skills. I have only one good eye, which has 20/20 vision, so I am a meritorious lip reader.

"When you are speaking to Isaiah, I observe your facial expressions and lip movement. I know what you are saying even before Isaiah signs to me. This will come as naturally to the children as any speaking conversation could ever be."

Joshua told Isaiah to tell me that the children observed Isaiah and me in sign, and many speaking children sign what they have picked up just by watching us. Their favorite sign is, "I love you."

I then asked Joshua, "What do you require of me?"

Joshua and Mr. Miller responded that they would prefer for me to continue to learn their ways. "Teach the children acceptable behavior, basic discipline, and respect for others; continue your belief in God, study His Word as you are now doing, obey His precepts, and give Him your whole heart and service. We believe, if you do this, your teaching will convince us. We are already pleased you are modest in your dress and we request you continue to be conscious of it."

Mr. Miller looked at me directly all the time he was talking and stated, "I have observed Isaiah talking to you in sign and am pleased how quickly he has learned your language and translates it back to us with so much facial expression and emotion. His ability shows you have taught him well and we would be pleased to have you teach our children! Will you accept this position?"

"I will be pleased and honored to teach the children. Thank you for the opportunity! I will personally receive more teaching from them than I will ever be able to give!"

The school board chairman's request to me was that I sign him as Josey and, if in the company of the students, Mr. Miller. I agreed. When the meeting ended, I asked Isaiah to take the rest of my box of books and bring them to my bedroom, where I could sort the ones I would use for teaching. I was excited and looking forward to beginning the very next day.

I awoke to a killing frost covering the land and back roads, so I dressed warm, not knowing how warm or cold the school room would be.

When Isaiah and I arrived at school, we were earlier than the children, which gave us time to unpack and get settled. Fortunately, someone had arrived prior to us, so the stove was fired up and the room was warm and comfortable. The one-room school contained desks and a blackboard. The center of the room had a bar across it with curtains opening in the center. The purpose was to separate the room into two classrooms. Grades one through four were in the front part of the school room and grades five through eight were in the back. To the left was a small area with desks next to the curtains. This area was to be the special education area for me and my students. A portion of the blackboard was left empty for me to use for things I will teach.

The children arrived and there were three of them to start: Anna Troyer, 10 years old, and Levi Mast and Evonne Raber, both 13 years old. I thought to myself, with only three children, this will not be too difficult. I started by placing the alphabet sign up on the wall and this is where we began. I made paper apples with their names on them and made one for myself as well. We finger spelled their names until they knew them. By the end of the day, the children knew the alphabet, could finger spell their names and the names of common animals, like cat, dog, and horse. This first day went by quickly and I was pleased with the students' progress.

On Friday, Isaiah informed me we are going to the flea market in Shipshewana. This market began in the 1920s as a livestock auction. Then came consignments of miscellaneous items, eventually growing into a two-day event with multiple vendors and products. The Shipshewana auction and flea market drew large crowds, with just as many tourists who came to see the Amish way of life: food, dress, buggies, horses, and the culture.

Isaiah explained, "We do not like to have our pictures taken. We believe it to be prideful."

I noted the Amish people, as they arrived by horse and buggy. Many tourists were gazing at us and attempting to take our picture. Isaiah instructed me to turn my head away when they tried to snap a photo. He went on to say that, someday, tourism is going to take over. We enjoyed our day together – a grand, special day!

Chapter 16

Pennsylvania Dutch

When Isaiah took me to school on Monday, I was prepared for the day's lesson. Upon greeting Anna, Evonne, and Levi, I signed, "I love you." The speaking children in the classroom were signing it, as well, and laughing with one another as they ran out the door.

Isaiah picked me up after school and signed, "Collie, you will want to learn some German, too. In church, we speak Pennsylvania Dutch, as I had mentioned before. If you want, I will sign you some words and, thereby, will be your teacher."

I agreed to learn and we set aside one hour each evening, Monday through Thursday, for me to begin.

Four weeks later, on Saturday, Isaiah signed, "Collie, we are going to an Amish restaurant, 'The Eating Place,' in Middlebury, Indiana. It was built in 1970 and opened in 1971."

It looked like a large barn!

Isaiah signed, "They have made many additions over the years and it now has a bakery, country art gallery, assorted gift shops, and a full-staffed restaurant. Amish quilts are also sold here. It is now a major tourist attraction. In the summer, many English people come from many states. My purpose for bringing you here is for you to practice reading the lips of the Pennsylvania Dutch language. Although we have been practicing for nearly a month, it will be different for you at first. By paying close attention, you will start to make sense of some of the words."

We enjoyed a luncheon of chicken and noodles, applesauce, and vegetables. Every table had homemade apple butter and peanut butter – what a treat! I watched the Amish conversations and, true to Isaiah's word, I was able to pick up a few words. Isaiah assured me we would return again and see the unconstrained work of the Amish in other shops. I took pleasure in the day and looked forward to returning again.

After six weeks of teaching, the children were progressing very well. Two additional children joined the class: Esther Frey and Marlin Luthy.

So much in my class is visual and we were at the point where we could pair off two-by-two. This allowed me to spend one-on-one time with each student. I was astonished at how quickly the children learned! I had taught adults previously and they were quick to use signs, but these children were like sponges, soaking up and retaining everything! Their writing skills still required a lot of improvement, and I had to remind myself that their rapid learning of signs would not be as useful until they knew how to write to their family members. Only then would other family members understand what their children needed.

The signing form of communication was intricate in itself and I had to slow down so all aspects of learning could be retained. After a period of time, the other non–handicapped children became used to us, so I was able to open the curtain separating us from them, and they were able to concentrate on their learning without being annoyed by our hands flying around.

When the children went outside for recess, the other teacher, Lizzy Farmwald, and I went out with them. It was cold outside, so we were back inside in the warmth within 10 minutes. School ended for the day and I began to clean the classroom. Isaiah came by to pick me up and said he had a surprise for me.

When we went up the lane toward the house, I noticed a car in the drive. I approached the steps and Christine came flying out the door, nearly knocking me over!

She looked wonderful and we hugged and cried. Isaiah came up the steps and we all signed and shared our happy moments together. The door then opened and Christine's boyfriend came out smiling. She introduced him as Paul Johnson, her husband. I could not believe she was married! I signed to her, "Christine, where, when, for how long? Why didn't you write me about your marriage? We had exchanged letters this past year and you never mentioned this happy occasion."

"Collie, slow down! We just got married a couple of weeks ago and I wanted to surprise you in person."

Paul and Isaiah were quickly becoming acquainted, as he had spent most of the afternoon with them prior to my arriving from school. Paul signed that Christine had taught him to sign, as they have been together for quite some time. Paul could also communicate with Isaiah's and his family verbally.

Both Christine and Paul were charmed by Isaiah's family. Deborah and the girls prepared a wonderful meal and my friends were asked to stay. Isaiah and I showed them the farm and the four of us walked all over enjoying the brisk, cold air.

Later, we went in the house and Joshua began our evening prayer. Christine signed to me the next day, "Collie, you are right where God intends for you to be. Are you and Isaiah getting serious?"

"Isaiah and I are friends only," I shared. "My heart still flutters at the sight of him, but we are not of the same culture. Remember, I am a woman who has been molested! His family is not aware of any of this. Neither is Isaiah. He will meet a young woman of his people, who he will spend his life with, and they will have many children and live here forever."

Christine signed, "This makes me sad for you because you are an amazing woman, and I can tell you have strong feelings for him. You have also become equally attached to his family. I can see he is fond of you as well. It seems so unfair that you cannot be together! Collie, have the two of you even discussed the possibility of dating and perhaps marriage?"

"We are just friends, Christine, and that means more to me than you can imagine. Someday, I hope to marry, but our lives are not alike. Let us change the subject! Please tell me you are still as captivated by your career as you always were."

"Paul and I have had some wonderful experiences these past years with our careers. At present, we are concentrating more on his career than mine. We have been dauntless in our efforts for him to succeed. Eventually, we hope to have a family, but I will be content with my standing in life as his wife until the time comes for God to bless us with children. At present, though, we will continue to advance his career. I want to tell you, Collie, that there is a young, deaf woman who has made many movies and is being recognized more than I ever hoped to be. She is going to open doors for many with our handicap."

"Where are you and Paul living?"

"We are living in the Gig Harbor area of Washington State for now. It is close to Seattle. However, if Paul continues to surpass what he is doing and is recognized at most movie events we attend, we may relocate to Hollywood, California, where most movies are made. We are trusting in God to open the doors and direct us in His plan."

We visited until late in the evening, then Paul and Christine went into Shipshewana to a bed and breakfast home they had reserved earlier in the day. Isaiah signed, "I made arrangements with Paul for us to go to Middlebury again, to 'The Eating Place.' I know they will enjoy the atmosphere and delicious food. They will pick us up in their automobile tomorrow."

When they picked us up the next day, I was nervous. It had been a long time since I had ridden in an automobile. I felt like we were traveling too fast and would backend an Amish horse and buggy. Paul was a good driver, though, and that eased my mind. I could not believe how accustomed I had become to commuting slowly by horse and buggy.

As predicted, Paul and Christine were elated by the life of the people and the land I had come to love. One of their biggest surprises was the fact that I was living without electricity and took pleasure in the sights, smells, dress, and simple life. Though they appreciated the simple style of dress and the horse-drawn buggies, they just could not grasp the ways of the Old Order Amish, especially not having a light switch on the wall or an inside bathroom!

I signed to Christine, "They have so much with so little, they have no need for more. My only explanation is they trust in God for everything. Their faith is everything you always wanted for me. They have demonstrated that it brings an answer to prayer, guidance, stability, and, most of all, salvation! I could go on and on, and I know you tried to make me understand this many years ago. You wanted me to believe in God and I rejected Him. Now I have confirmation! I am still daily learning His ways – that they are not my ways. The longer I remain here, the more I understand what you wanted for me. Isaiah and his family have provided me with acceptance and security, and I could not be happier with my surroundings."

The next day, Paul and Christine prepared to leave. We exchanged addresses so we could continue to write, with no promise of when we would meet again. We cried and signed our love for one another. She expressed, again, her delight with my progress and embracing search to love and honor the Lord. She also encouraged me to consider my feelings for Isaiah and let him know I have feelings for him. As they pulled away from the farm, I saw Christine's arm come out of the car window with the "I love you" sign. I returned the sign right back to her as they drove out of sight.

That night, in my room, I sat down and wrote her a long letter. I explained that when I had been attacked years ago and lost my virginity to the man who molested me, I could not come to Isaiah as a pure woman. I was also not of the Amish culture. Amish men do not marry outside of their culture and they live among their people. I waited for a couple of weeks, and, with a sorrowful heart, mailed the letter.

Chapter 17

Deer Hunting

The signing routine at school was picking up at a faster pace. The children informed me their parents and siblings were learning from one another and signing at home. This was encouraging to me, as it would help them to sign better. This would also make them feel good to be the teacher instead of the student.

Isaiah brought me to school one morning and checked to make sure the fire was going well before he left. Before the children arrived, I returned to the woodshed to get a couple more pieces of wood, as it was very cold outside. I didn't bother to bring the kerosene lantern with me and a sharp snap at my fingertips made me jump! Then I remembered there were many small traps for the little critters – they loved to play with the toilet paper in there! I was happy my fast fingertip reaction allowed me to escape injury. I felt a little nervous when I returned to the classroom and made a mental note to have an older boy check the woodshed for critters. I believed today would be a good day despite the incident with my fingertip. Recess, however, proved differently!

It was cold and rainy, but we still played catch in a circle. The ball hit Anna in the face, so recess ended early. I commenced to clean Anna up and console her when I looked up and noted the other two scholars had their hands flying in sign, protesting the short recess, and were not ready to come in. I got their attention when I challenged them to guess what I found on the way to the outhouse. They became so eager to find out what it was, they forgot about recess. This is where they learned the simple sign for mouse. Suddenly, and for the rest of the day, Levi had to go to the outhouse. This made me smile and somehow made the whole day go just right, despite the rain, cold, and the critters in the woodshed.

Isaiah had been teaching his family sign. I was so happy! Rebekah signed to me that she would like me to learn quilting. We would still have to write notes to communicate, but it was imminent that some signs would be learned by them. I had noticed that Deborah, Ruth, and Leah were enjoying signing to one another. When they became confused, I helped them and we laughed at their mistakes.

I had begun the habit of putting my hand over my mouth when I laughed because, early in life, I found the noise I made was annoying to others. They never seemed to mind, however, and I would almost forget to cover my mouth! They asked me if I had a favorite sign and I signed, "I love you." They quickly agreed and walked around the house signing it to each other. I showed them the sign for God, Jesus, and the sentence, "I love you, God."

At school the next day, I began with prayer. Then, I began to prepare the students with more solid grounding in the basics: reading, writing, and arithmetic. The older children, Eli and Evonne, were eager to help Esther, Marlin, and Anna, and I was pleased with their overall progress. Being deaf, we are not distracted by voices, other noises, or singing.

Lizzie, the other teacher, gave me words to a song, and I read her lips and signed the words over and over until I understood when to sign each. The scholars learned this same technique as well, but the progress was much slower. They are just now beginning to feel the vibration from music as I have always felt it. We must practice this often to achieve the desired effects of lip reading and signing, connecting it to music. It is such a joy for me to receive the blessings of the students using the signs and skills they are being taught. Their adoring rosy cheeks and smiles radiated into my heart! The blessings are obvious and the pleasure I was feeling delighted my soul.

German was difficult for me to learn. Lip reading in German was more of a struggle then I could have ever imagined. Considering the only language I have ever been taught was English, I guess this is to be expected with any foreign language. Isaiah signed the word "Vertrauen" in German over and over and I became discontented and fidgety.

It means, "Trust, faith (confidence), Collie," he signed. "You must continue to try and learn. Stop twitching in your chair and practice!"

Needless to say, or sign, I was becoming very upset. I could not hear his tone of voice, but I could see him unsettled. He was very perceptive, which made it worse.

"That is enough, Isaiah. I will see you tomorrow. Goodnight!"

Teaching is easier when you know what you're teaching. Learning, however, is not. I asked God to bring that to mind when I am in school with the children. I also asked forgiveness for being saucy with Isaiah. Tomorrow, I will apologize.

The next day, Rebekah signed, "The men went hunting. They will bring back a deer and we will eat it this winter."

I signed, "I have never eaten deer, is it good?"

She nodded yes and smiled. She wrote me a note and said, "I believe you will like it a lot." Then she wrote asking if I would like to learn to quilt.

The mending I had done did not prepare me for the rigorous fine stitches required in quilting. She already had many squares cut out, but she patiently showed me how to measure, pin, and lay out a pattern of choice. I was creating something as foreign as the German and Pennsylvania Dutch languages Isaiah was teaching me. The tranquility I received from this was so salient that I didn't want to stop. However, it was time to prepare lunch, so I laid aside my work and helped Rebekah and the girls cook. "When will the men return?" I asked. I was feeling ashamed of my previous behavior toward Isaiah and wanted to apologize.

The men returned and, after we had eaten, I asked Isaiah in sign if we could go for a walk. He agreed.

The sky was dark as we left the barn, and the falling snow was beautiful as it touched the ground. It got colder, so I was ready to go back inside to the warmth of the family awaiting us for evening prayer.

Upon return to the house, I signed, "Isaiah, I want to apologize for my behavior last evening. I behaved like a spoiled child!"

He smiled in his genteel manner and assured me of his forgiveness. He then took me around to the barn and showed me two deer hanging. I thought I would faint! They were hanging by two ropes thrown over the rafters and tied by their hind legs. Their stomachs were split open with a stick going from side to side inside their stomachs.

"I don't think I will ever be able to eat them!"

"Collie, we will process our deer and have many meals from them. You will like them!"

I think back and know Christine knew then what I am just beginning to understand. Isaiah was and is more important to me than I even realize. My feeling for him was difficult to keep from expressing, yet I didn't know what he was feeling about me and was afraid to find out. My attention was drawn back to what he was signing, "Thanksgiving is coming soon and we will have venison to feast on, among many other delicious foods."

This Sunday we did not have church, so the men returned to hunting and the ladies all quilted. I was learning quickly at how many hands working together could produce such a beautiful quilt. The men came back and, once again, they had two more deer.

Isaiah signed, "The first two the other day were bucks (male) and these are does (female)."

We took our late afternoon walk and Isaiah signed, "It is getting colder, Collie. Are you warm enough in your bedroom?"

"The quilts keep me quite warm."

As we signed to one another, Isaiah looked up and pointed to the sky, "A while back a flight of Tundra Swans were passing through. They are called Whistling Swans. It seemed like hundreds passed through that day! The big white swans migrate through and may choose to spend the winter here. They were forced to fly at lower altitudes because of the strong crosswinds."

We walked the large pond behind the home and Isaiah signed, "The native Indiana bird is called a Mute Swan. They do not whistle like the Tundra Swans."

"They are all mute to me, Isaiah!"

He smiled down at me and placed his arm across my shoulder. He understood.

I signed, "Is your hearing getting worse or the same?"

"A little worse, but I still hear the Tundra Swans whistle. As November draws to a close, most of the waterfowl will go south. Enjoy this season; it is another of God's creation!"

As we walked back to the house, I reflected over what Isaiah signed: another of God's creation and the beauty of it.

Chapter 18

Marriage Customs

Often it is the small things in a relationship that make a difference, i.e. men hunting for food, planting a garden, creating a quilt, learning to listen with sign, and lip reading. These things may not seem like much, but, over time, they serve to build a strong relationship.

I thought about my move here and wondered will I marry? Or, am I always to be alone? I know God knows I struggle with tough decisions, but I am finally learning to seek Him and His wisdom. I am actively seeking a firm relationship with Him and His will. The rest of my life without God is simply skubala (manure). That is what the Bishop calls it anyway!

We had a wonderful day together and, even if I could talk, the quietness between us would still have been there. There was no need for words or signs between two friends enjoying friendship and peace.

Joshua came in and told Rebekah there will be a wedding the Thursday before Thanksgiving. Sara Weaver met Andrew Yoder from Elkhart, Indiana, about a year ago. They decided in June to marry and just announced it this week.

Andrew works at the trailer factory. He and Sara met at church at the Bontrager home. This doesn't give Rebekah much time to help, as it's only two weeks away! I signed to Rebekah that I wanted to help. It will be my first time to attend a wedding here. I also wondered if they decided to be married in June, why is everyone just finding out now.

With Isaiah's help, Rebekah signed, "The family knew of their intentions in June, however, the Amish community is usually not told until one month before the wedding takes place. Then the engagement is announced in church. Here again, each Amish District varies in announcing upcoming marriages. Most Amish weddings take place in November or December, after the harvesting season is over. Tuesdays and Wednesdays are popular days of the week to marry because a full day before and after are needed to prepare for the wedding, and this can never include Sunday! The day before is dedicated to helping prepare food for the celebration by the married couple.

I signed, "Since I am not a part of the married couple's family, what am I to do to help?" I was told that usually, unless you are Amish, you cannot attend the wedding, but you can attend the reception. "I do not want to intrude on this special day."

Rebekah signed, "You will work with me in preparing the food and will attend the wedding with us. This is one of the special days when men help the women in the kitchen. Isaiah will also help. The reception normally begins around noon after the wedding. We will find out what the bride wants to be served. It will be a very busy day and you will feel exhausted when we are finished."

Lizzie was having trouble with one of her fourth-grade students today at school. The boy was mischievous, so she took him aside and reprimanded him. I saw his lips form the words he hated her. Make no mistake, my lip reading is exact and I was sure of what he said. I spoke to her at recess and asked if I could help somehow. She nodded no and mouthed for me to read that as "thank you, but no. I will manage."

After recess, I noticed she had changed his seat to the front row. After school, she made him stay and sweep the floor. He kept staring at her and finally put the broom down and said, "Miss Farmwald, I do not hate you and am sorry I said that. I know you were right to correct me for saying bad things to Eli and I will be better tomorrow." With that, she hugged him and told him she had forgiven him!

After the children left and Lizzie and I were alone, she wrote on a piece of paper, "I love them and want to be a good teacher. I make mistakes, also, and am as human as they. Tonight I am tired and feel like I could cry." I put my arms around her and that seemed to be all she needed to comfort her.

I signed to Isaiah that night, "If Amish women don't teach, how do they make money? I know being self-sufficient and working hard is important. I have witnessed the self-reliance and hard work in the home and garden, cooking, sewing, gardening, washing, and raising children."

Isaiah signed, "Amish women have been successful in selling their homemade quilts, canned goods, floral arrangements, toys, and baked goods. But I maintain the most self-supporting business for Amish women is the quilting business. You will be amazed once you get out to the shops more often and see how many people come from all over the world to visit and buy their beautiful handcrafted quilts. Some quilts sell for $2,000 or more. The reason being is they are made from hand, and stitching and sewing are an art. The Amish will buy simple clothes, but not the tourist. They prefer fancy.

"Homemade dolls sell well, also, and so do home-canned fruits and vegetables and jams and jellies from our own gardens. Restaurants and bakeries will also buy homemade breads, pies, cakes, noodles, cookies and candy."

I signed, "How do the women find time for God and to perform all of the aforementioned tasks?"

"They still have time to place God first. Their days are long and being a wife and mother is very demanding. You know, Collie, even with your handicap, you are amazing as well! You find time to teach, prepare your lessons, help my family, and still give of yourself to everyone you meet. You find a way to communicate and make everyone happy around you. I often see you give notes to my mem to see what you can do to help her. You have an abundance of energy and I admire that in you."

"Since my arrival here, I do not notice my handicap as much. Everyone has tried hard to learn my sign. Communication is far better than anywhere I have ever lived in the past. It is pleasing for me to help in any way I can! Approval is very important to me. Without it, I would fail in many aspects of the teaching world."

When I awoke the next morning, it was bitter cold and had snowed overnight. Isaiah and I went to school to get the classroom heated and ready for the day. Isaiah shoveled a path to the outhouse and a path back to the school and up two steps into the building. Joshua brought Deborah, Ruth, and Leah later. I decided, after prayer, to begin the day with math. The children were learning to add and subtract, so I brought a jar of beans and decided to give 10 to each. They counted out five and gave them to a partner, then signed the remainder to me. I had to work hands-on with the children since I was the sixth person.

Chapter 19

The Five Senses

We often worked in pairs and in two groups. We would trade around so I could be with each child and teach them. Math is difficult for children and when Levi, Evonne, Esther, and Marlin had to work with fractions, signing could make it more arduous.

When we got ready for recess, Miss Farmwald noticed two deer outside. She asked for quiet! We all quietly went out to the playground and watched them. I noticed their big, beautiful, dark eyes, with their white tails twitching back and forth. I signed to the children, "God's wild creatures are keen in their senses."

Earlier we had learned about the five senses, so I asked them to watch their ears go forward and backward as they heard us come out the door. I told them to watch how the deer stopped everything to listen. We only stood there for a couple of minutes when their sense of smell detected us and they scampered off into the woods. All we could see were their white tails.

After recess was over, we returned to the classroom. Once again, we reviewed our five senses and each signed to me how their sense of sight had helped in near-tragic situations in the past.

At lunch time, Anna wanted to share her lunch with me. I thanked her but declined, as I was not hungry. I then realized she wanted me to help eat her lunch so she could quickly return outside to see if the deer had returned. All of the children spent their lunchtime with an abundance of high-energy, running games. I began to think back about the schools in Fort Wayne and if the people who graduated could be transported back in time to their childhood times of the 1950s. It may well compare to the Amish schools of the late 1980s or early 1990s.

I set the spelling words up for the afternoon instruction. I looked over at Lizzie's classroom area and she was preparing an arithmetic lesson for the children to learn. I put on my coat to go outside and help retrieve the students. The wind had picked up and Anna was looking toward the woods for the deer. I signed to her that maybe they were cold and wanted to go back to the warmth of the trees blocking the wind. Finally, she turned back for one last glance and ran back into the school.

I was still studying Pennsylvania Dutch and it was not easy for me.

Isaiah reminded me, "I learned High German from the time I was a small child. You cannot expect to learn quickly. Relax and enjoy the lessons! You are doing well and are signing the words to my family in English; and then you sign them back to me. As I give you the sentences for tonight, you can practice for as long as you need. I learned the High German by hearing and seeing it written on paper as well.

"You will learn Pennsylvania Dutch, as it is much easier than High German. Since you do not have the benefit of hearing, I will try and form the words on my lips clearly so you will understand. Is it easier the way we have been doing it, or is it easier to do it only on paper?"

I signed, "The way you are now teaching me is satisfactory."

Isaiah responded, "You will find that the future will have you using Pennsylvania Dutch more often than English once you learn it. Church will be clearer to you as you read the Bishop's lips and share the Word of God. Some parents allow their 10- to 14-year-old children to write and play in church. A few mothers claim they are taking notes. I believe some children miss most of what is being said and don't benefit from the sermon as much. Some ministers believe that when children go to school they are too old for pencil and paper in church. However, if you use this method to learn the Pennsylvania Dutch, Collie, then that is okay. If you're using the method to learn language, you can decide what is best to serve your needs."

When we finished the lesson, we went into the kitchen for prayer time. Rebekah signed, "Collie, I spoke to Sara Weaver this week. She is planning her wedding-day meal. She has decided on fried chicken, cheese, bread and butter, applesauce, jelly, fruitcakes, and pie and ice cream. The wedding will take place in Sara's home. There will be an early morning church service, where she and Andrew will exchange vows. As I mentioned before, it will be a busy day, but we will still be able to enjoy ourselves."

"Thank you, again, for including me. I am honored to be a part of the festivities."

Rebekah signed, "Sara will be a winsome bride."

Rebekah made a shoofly pie for supper so when we returned from the auction barn in Topeka we could have some. I had been thinking about the pie and signed to Isaiah, "Why is your mem's pie called shoofly pie?"

"There are various explanations and some say it is a French recipe – that the crumb topping resembled the surface of a cauliflower, which the French pronounced chou-fleur, pronounced in English as shoofly. The logical explanation, however, seems to be that the sweet ingredient attracted flies. When the pies were cooking, they swarmed around and the cooks had to 'shoo' the flies away."

This last explanation makes more sense, as the pies are very sweet. The Pennsylvania Dutch claims this pie as "their very own creation," because, in the early years, sorghum was used. Mem used brown sugar and molasses, which makes them pleasing to the palate!

As I looked out over the fields at the snow falling, I thought of the warm bread smell coming from the oven and the warmth of the house. I was looking forward to the encounter with the shoofly pie tonight.

"I received a letter from Jeanna and Kevin, my dear friends from Fort Wayne. They are expecting a baby in May. Kevin's mother died and he inherited her house. They have a small yard for the baby and future babies to come. They want me to visit. I will write back and let them know my decision."

Isaiah signed, "It may have to be in the spring, when the baby is close to being born, as the weather will be getting worse. Thanksgiving and Christmas will be coming and a lot of activity will be going on. If you feel the need to visit them, Collie, I will try to make arrangements with Bill, the driver who brought you here – only if this meets with your approval."

"Thank you," I signed. "We will see what the winter brings for driving conditions."

Chapter 20

The Wedding

Sara's wedding day was fast approaching and we were very, very busy! Wednesday morning, the day before the wedding, Joshua, Isaiah, Amos, Jacob, even Joseph, assisted Andrew, the groom, and his parents and brothers.

All of the women were in the kitchen preparing food for the wedding. On Thursday, the day of the wedding, we were all gathered at Sara's home, and an early morning church service was held. With an exception made for me, Isaiah and I sat off to the side so he could sign the wedding vows. The Bishop presided over them, counseling them and making sure they fully understood the permanence of the ceremony and the vows, because divorce is not allowed in the Amish community. There was a reading from the hymnals, Scripture was read, and a long sermon followed. Andrew and Sara made their vows, they were blessed, and a final prayer was said. Afterwards, around noon time, the party and feasting began.

We had an abundance of food that was set up around the perimeter of the largest room in Sara's parent's house. A special table was set up in the corner for the bridal party. Sara sat to the left of Andrew. In some Districts this might symbolize where she will sit in the marriage buggy. The single women sat on the bride's side of the room and the single Amish men sat on the groom's side. Both parents and siblings sat together in the kitchen.

The remainder of the afternoon was spent talking, singing, and game playing.

Rebekah, with the help of Isaiah, signed, "Collie, sometimes an Amish wedding is used as an opportunity for match-making between teenagers who are over the age of 16. They are assigned specific seats before the evening meal time in order to bring them closer together. Not many gifts are given, usually just the closest family members or friends give practical gifts, such as Amish quilts, farming tools, and canned foods. A second meal will be served just before sundown. The bride, groom, and their parents sit in the middle room at the main table and the same type of food will be served again. Most Amish weddings will go late into the night. They will spend their first night in Sara's parent's home so they can help with cleanup the following morning."

I signed, "Will they go on a honeymoon as is the custom of the English?"

"No, it is customary that for the next several months they spend the night or weekend with different Amish members on both sides of the family in order for everyone to get to know one another better. During this time, they may receive gifts such as dishes, cookware, and other useful household items. Sara and Andrew will live with Sara's family the rest of the winter and begin to set up their new home in the spring. It is the Amish culture to have a dowry, which may include household furnishings. All of the acquired household items will be used to furnish the couple's new home."

I signed, "I admire the customs you have in your Amish culture. You help one another and take care of your families without the reliance on things of the world."

It was late when we finished the day and arrived home. I was more than fatigued and thankful we were on Thanksgiving break from school. I knew we were only one week away from Thanksgiving and a lot of preparation would be needed for the upcoming week.

Chapter 21

Thanksgiving

This morning, Joshua woke up with a fever and sore throat. He had contracted a cold and Rebekah is doctoring him as best she can. He is disappointed and upset, as he wanted to go deer hunting.

Rebekah signed, "We have a lot of canned deer and summer sausage already, and many of the jars contain chunked deer already prepared for homemade noodles stored in many canning jars put away for the winter. Joshua will just have to get over this cold before he goes back out hunting. Fish, chicken, and venison will feed us over the winter months satisfactorily. The chickens are doing quite well and we have plenty of eggs, and potatoes from the garden are stored, so we are very blessed."

My thought was it is no wonder Joshua is sick with this sleet and snow. Due to his workload, he is in the elements daily doing chores and deer hunting.

All of the men love to hunt, and this type of weather is ideal for preserving the meat until it is processed. The longer it hangs in the cold the more tender it will become. Even Deborah, Ruth, and Leah are anxious to hunt deer. Although Rebekah signed, "I believe Leah talks too much and hopes to scare the deer off so no one can shoot them. Ha, ha!"

We all laughed at that and Leah told us she wanted to bake and cook and not be a hunter. In sign, I agreed I would be woeful at seeing a deer shot and killed, even though I know it puts food on the table. I remembered the deer the children saw at school a few weeks ago and they are beautiful.

I signed to Rebekah, "I noticed that Sara did not wear a white dress for her wedding. Nor did she have an engagement or wedding ring. When my friends, Jeanna

and Kevin, exchanged vows at their wedding, they also exchanged rings, unlike Sara and Andrew."

Rebekah signed, "Sara wore a new, blue dress that will be worn again on other occasions. If you noticed, she also wore no makeup. She did not receive a ring because the Amish Order Ordnung (rules) prohibits personal jewelry. It is a way of managing individualism. In some District weddings, celery is one of the symbolic foods served, oftentimes placed in vases. This is to decorate the house instead of flowers. We do not do this in our District."

I signed, "This is uncommon to the English way. Isaiah already informed me that pictures are not permissible in order to avoid personal vanity. I am learning more each and every day about your customs and beliefs and how different we English are. Then I look at myself and see how different I am to the English-speaking people as well. I have lived in a world of silence and confusion all of my life. The Lord is reminding me more and more daily that I am no longer a victim of my circumstances."

Thanksgiving morning arrived. The turkey was killed and dressed and the food was prepared. The whole family gathered for devotions and each one of us shared what we are thankful for. Isaiah and I signed, and those in the family who had picked up the signing contributed to my understanding so I could share during the day. Joshua was thankful for God's blessings on his entire family and for the healing from his cold and fever. Rebekah was thankful for God's blessings on her family and the abundance of provisions for the winter months. Isaiah, Amos, Jacob, and Joseph were thankful for God's blessings and the successful hunting season they enjoyed. Deborah, Ruth, and Leah were thankful for God's blessings and for my presence among them and teaching them the language of sign. I was thankful for God's blessings and my presence among them and teaching the language of sign. I was also thankful for them making me an integral part of their family and lives.

The adults and older children had a separate time of prayer and then, around noon, we all gathered to share in the Thanksgiving meal. The meal consisted of turkey, dressing, mashed potatoes and gravy, vegetables, salads, freshly baked bread, and desserts. Upon completion of the meal, the adults visited with one another.

Since it was cold and snowing outside, the children chose to play games inside. I was watching them, smiling, as they began to play. Isaiah came over and sat beside me. He signed the game they were playing. The game was called "Peter, John, and I." Any number of players form a circle and the person who is "IT" stands in the center of the circle, blindfolded, holding a broom or yardstick. The rest walk around the circle until "IT" pounds his stick on the floor. At this signal, everyone stands perfectly still. "IT," then, reaches out with his stick and touches one of the children asking who it is. The victim says, "Peter, John and I," disguising their voice. If "IT" guesses who it is, then that person will replace the person in the circle. If they don't guess correctly, then the game continues as before. The older children catch on quickly and don't remain in the circle very long, but it is much more difficult for the younger ones.

I signed, "It looks like fun, but I never played many games growing up."

It was getting late and I was getting tired. The children grabbed my hand to play the game, but, sadly, I had to remind them I was deaf and only a few of them could sign. However, it was pleasing that they had forgotten about my deafness and wanted me to join them!

The next day, I received a Thanksgiving card from Christine and Paul. I signed part of it to Isaiah's family. "Paul and I send our blessings to all of you. We hope to come back to see you after the winter season passes, perhaps in late spring or early summer." After signing that part to them, I continued on to read the remainder to myself.

Paul was co-starring in another movie. Christine was pleased for his talents to be recognized. It gave me pleasure that Christine was not prideful, or I would have read it in her letter. Nor was she a talebearer of the society she lived in. It would be very easy for her, though, as she knows we don't hear the news of the worldly rich and famous. She only mentioned one statement to me that was of concern. Due to her deafness, some people in that society were not eager or comfortable to be around her. Sometimes Paul would attend a party in one of the producer's homes without her. I fleetingly wondered if it bothered her to not attend with him.

She sounded happy and eager to share all of the California scenery, including the Pacific Ocean view they enjoyed every day from their home. I remembered her dream to become a star one day, and she was living her dream through Paul. Tonight I would pray for them, as I did every night. Right now, though, I felt drawn to pray for her only, as I have over the years. I missed my friend!

Chapter 22

The Scholars

Isaiah's brother, Joseph, came home tonight upset that Amos broke his foot. They were playing football and he got hurt. The doctor had to put a plate and screw in it, so he will be laid up for six weeks or longer. It seems the snow was falling pretty hard and he slipped and somehow landed wrong. However, he was bothered more by the accident he saw on the way home. A truck hit a horse. The horse went through the windshield and only the hind legs were sticking out. There was a great deal of blood and innards spilled everywhere, and the passengers in the truck were covered in blood. They used another truck to pull the horse out to free them. Thank God no human was injured or killed! It's just another reminder that cars and trucks and horses and buggies are a dangerous combination on the highways. The brothers are still shaking from the dreadful accident and the possibility of lives lost!

I welcomed returning to school on Monday, which was cold and windy. The scholars had a wonderful Thanksgiving program on Wednesday before Thanksgiving break. They signed a song and the speaking children sang. They thanked God for all they have. Parents enjoyed their time with us at school that evening.

After prayer, we settled into reading, writing, spelling, and arithmetic. Miss Farmwell wrote me a note to say the children are so loud today. "It is too cold to go outside, so will your people join us in a quiet game called '7 Up?'"

I smiled, nodded my head, and signed to the scholars, "Are you familiar with the game '7 Up?'"

They signed in return, "Yes!"

I signed to Evonne, "Please explain to me how the game is played."

Evonne signed, "Seven children stand at the front of the room while the rest sit with their heads down on their desks. The seven students each tap one person on the head and return to their places at the front. To prevent one person from getting two taps, the students raise their hands when they are tapped. When everyone is back, one person up front says, '7 Up.' Everyone then looks up and the seven who are tapped take turns guessing who tapped them. If they guess correctly, they exchange places. If the guess is not correct, the person who tapped remains up front."

I signed, "This is a nice game to play when you want quiet, because talking is not allowed while the tapping is being done."

I now understood why Miss Farmwald wrote on the paper that the pupils were loud. All I could see and feel coming from her classroom was laughter and hands pounding the desks. My scholars are always quiet, as they have learned the art of hearing is available to anyone, even to those whose eardrums do not respond to sound waves. Even though they are young, they have gained insight into something very beautiful. Each word is said in a very distinct way and hand and fingers move in perfect rhythm, thereby forming speech into an art that brings hearing to the truly deaf.

The flu bug made its way into the school and two of my five students were absent this week. I concentrated on helping little Anna with her sign reading. She is only six years old and has improved with the help of other scholars.

Due to the inclement weather, we played a game inside during recess one day called "You Know." We sat around the table with hands overlapping. I began slapping Anna's left hand down on the table, then she slapped mine in return. Two slaps means reverse. If we lose count or mess up, the game is over and the other one wins. I liked to play it with students. After the game, we went directly into multiple subjects.

Holding up a basket, I signed, "How many eggs?"

Anna counted three. I continued to switch and she kept up well. I switched for her to sign, "How old are you?"

"Six."

Then I asked her to sign John 3:16, where Jesus was born, the name of a sandwich, and, finally, the word horse. She did quite well and it was soon time to go home. Another week of school and I was enjoying teaching more than I ever expected.   Isaiah reminded me that we would practice Pennsylvania Dutch again. I was happy to revert back to the student again and even enjoyed learning the new language I thought I would never understand.

I signed to Isaiah, "Sis kald heit."

He returned the sign, "It is cold today!" Then, "In's haus, fees kald?" (In the house, feet cold?)

I signed in return, "Nay."

We both laughed because he said I spoke with my lips reading in Pennsylvania Dutch, but we signed in English.

"This could become complex!" Isaiah signed. His animated expressions made me clap and laugh again.

We ended our lesson with hot coffee and waited for Isaiah's daed, Joshua, to begin our evening devotion. I was beginning to pick up the Pennsylvania Dutch language as he read the Bible and shared their beliefs.

Chapter 23

Rumspringa

Our monthly sewing ladies group gathered at Sara Zook's home. It was well attended, with around 12 women present. We worked on the quilts that will be given away at Christmas. I believe we counted 14 twin-size quilts, with four more to finish before Christmas. Our goal is 20, but we will be pleased with 18. This will please the nursing home residents to have new covers on their beds.

Rebekah signed to me as she rested from quilting, "Sara commented to us as we were creating the roses on the quilt, 'Truth and roses have thorns.'"

One of the other ladies said, "Right is still right if nobody does it, it is still wrong if everyone does it."

I signed back to Rebekah, "Jesus is a friend who walks in when the world has walked out."

What lovely smiles I noticed around the quilting circle when Rebekah repeated what I signed.

When we returned home, the sky was pitch black and the air was cold with freezing rain mixed with snow. It was 22 degrees and I was glad to be back in the warmth of my room!

I sat by my window, reflecting on the enlightenment God revealed to me this day, which I shared with the ladies, "Jesus is a friend who walked into my world when the world walked out." This phrase, without my foreknowledge of Jesus, has applied to me

throughout my life. I did not know when the world walked out on me, but I do know now that Jesus has walked in.

Today, after school, when Isaiah and I were coming home, in sign I told him I had read Deborah's lips and she was saying that Jacob was in Rumspringa. "Will you tell me about it?"

"It is a term meaning 'running around.' Usually the age begins at 16. In some Districts, girls could be as young as 14. It is when serious courtships begin and church rules are relaxed.

"As in non-Amish families, it is understood there will be a certain amount of misbehavior, although it is not encouraged or overlooked. The most common time for boy/girl get-togethers is the bi-weekly, Sunday evening sing. However, they will use sewing bees, frolics, and weddings for other times to see each other. The sing is often conducted at the same house or barn as the Sunday morning service. Many teens come from several Districts, because socialization on a wider scale is more visible than at a single church.

"After chores are over and on the day of the sing, Jacob will dress in his good clothes, making sure his buggy and horses are clean. His sister, or sister's friend, may ride with him, but not usually his girlfriend. At the sing, boys sit on one side of a long table, girls on the other. Each person chooses a hymn and only the faster ones are chosen. Jacob and others will talk between songs.

"The formal conclusion of the sing ends around 10:00, followed by joking, talking, and visiting. Then Jacob and the other boys who do not have girlfriends will pair up with a maidel (girl). Following this, the boy takes the girl home in his open-topped, courting buggy. At the end of this period, Amish young adults are baptized into the church and usually marry, with only church members' permission. A small percentage of young people will choose not to join the church, deciding to live the rest of their lives in the world and marry someone outside of the Amish community. The Amish are not allowed to marry a first cousin, and second-cousin relationships are frowned upon, though they may occur.

"During the Rumspringa, parents respect the privacy of the couple and what they do is not discussed among family or friends. Excessive teasing by me or Jacob's other brothers and sisters at the wrong time are considered invasive."

While we were discussing this, I wanted to know if Isaiah had a maidel, but I was almost sure he did not, because he was not married. In fact, I have never seen him with anyone!

"Collie, I began losing my hearing when I was around Joseph's age, 15. I did go through Rumspringa, but I never wanted to burden anyone with what I knew would become a handicap. I was timid and unsure of how rapidly my hearing might diminish. I resolved to not consider marriage for a while anyway. As the years have passed, I sense I may never marry."

When we arrived home, I pondered over our conversation and thanked God we are friends. Maybe I can be of more help to Isaiah as his hearing worsens. I thank God that he, his friends, and family have learned sign so communication will always be available to him.

Later that night, I awoke and smelled smoke. I jumped out of bed and saw from the window that the neighbor's barn was on fire. I could see many horses and buggies going towards their home. I quickly dressed and went downstairs. Rebekah signed that the men folk had pumped a lot of water into containers and put it in the wagon to take to the Souks' farm. We sat down and she signed a prayer for the family and the animals' lives to be spared.

"This is one of our fears, that fire will destroy our family's lives, the animals, and all of the feed and wagons. We turn this over to God to protect what we work for. He will provide us with the right people, who will work to rebuild. In the morning, we will make a lot of food, along with many other families. The men folk will work all night to salvage what they can and neighbors from many Districts will come to help."

When Joshua, Isaiah, and the men came home, they looked worn out and smelled of smoke. They reported that all of the animals but one workhorse survived.

Chapter 24

Hard Work

After the fire subsided, the men rested for about two hours, at which time the horses, buggies, and wagons returned to the Souks' farm to continue the work. Rebekah had about 15 women helping in her kitchen to prepare food, and 20 or more were in the Souks' kitchen doing the same. The older children helped in watching and caring for the younger children. Everyone had a job to do and no one complained about what needed to be done.

The night air was cold, with temperatures in the low 20s. As morning arrived, temperatures rose to the high 40s. Even with the severe weather, everyone worked to restore the value of their lives. This value is defined by the desire to identify an appropriate standard that remains Amish: God will provide for all of their needs and they are to help their fellow man and bring glory to God. Rebekah signed to me, "The Bishop said we must never question God."

As the days passed there seemed to be 20 to 25 men working to rebuild the barn. The actual day of the barn raising occurred 10 days to two weeks later. It was a joyful day indeed! There was a great deal of food, laughter, praise to God, and a co-mingling of loving and caring family and friends. One of the families provided a workhorse to the

Souks and brought hay, straw, and feed. All of the saved animals were returned and, once again, all was well with the Souk family.

The next day, Isaiah and I went over to see the new barn. The smell of new wood and fresh hay were pleasing to me and I gained more insight into how God does provide.

After this latest crisis, life returned to normal once again. School was very busy with Miss Farmwald out sick. Another young teacher, Miss Sadie Yoder, filled in and was very good with the scholars. She and I were able to work out a recess arrangement —she would take the scholars out in the morning and I would take them out in the afternoon.

Due to the high snow drifts, we decided on a free-for-all snowball fight with rules. We would play an organized game with scholars choosing sides and forming lines within a good throwing distance from one another. There were limit lines they had to stay behind. When the throwing began and a player was hit three times, they were won over to the other side. The object was to dodge the snowballs as well as hitting the opponents. The side that had the most players when the bell rang won the contest. They returned to the classroom tired and the heat made them sleepy after being in the cold. I usually chose spelling lessons after recess, because they liked spelling and handwriting, but reading made them more sleepy.

Chapter 25

The Quilting Ladies

Christmas was rapidly approaching. Miss Lizzie Farmwald returned to school after being absent for one week from the flu. She had the scholars practicing Christmas songs and recitals of poetry. I had my scholars signing the real meaning of Christmas with simple songs and self-written poems. They also worked on drawings and spelling they could display in the classroom. Their signing helped them overcome shyness and learn to take an active part in family gatherings. Lizzie's pupils learned memorization, singing, teamwork, and cooperation in preparing it all, so we felt we would be ready for the Christmas program in a couple of weeks.

Joshua and Rebekah had begun their preparations for Christmas in their home. Homemade slippers, quilts, gloves, and numerous other items were being made for everyone. Many of these items were crafted after the children and men folk had retired for the evening. I was proud I had become a practiced quilter and knitter. My sewing was improving as well. I enjoyed working with Rebekah. She was accurately signing to me and we anticipated each other's thoughts at times.

Any confusion in communication that arose was when Rebekah and I wrote to each other in Pennsylvania Dutch. We shared a great deal of humor in our sign. We laughed and shook our heads at the men when they came in. They were always hungry and we were acting like we forgot how to cook since we were so busy. We knew we could make their stomach's happy, so we got up, set the table, and brought out a meal that would make men folk happy.

Rebekah informed me in sign, "The way to a man's heart is through his stomach."

I joyfully decided I wanted to become a great cook!

It was one week before Christmas and our monthly sewing ladies group completed the quilts. Rebekah signed for me to go with her and Sara Souk to deliver them to a nursing home in LaGrange, Indiana, the following day. I was delighted and happy to go and knew we would give much pleasure and warmth to the residents, as it did for all of us to sew them. I really enjoyed how we had grown in our friendships together.

For the Amish, hard work and determination is just a way of life, so 20 single quilts were completed and our goal was achieved. To some Amish Districts, there is an expression that all Amish children, at a very young age, learn. The meaning of JOY stands for their belief that Jesus comes first, others are in between, and you are last. What this means to Amish quilters, Rebekah signed, is no matter how tired you might be after the chores are done, you still have a responsibility to help others before you consider your own wants and needs. Whether it's your family or another, if they want a quilt to keep them warm, it's your duty to find time to make it.

Chapter 26

No Santa Claus

Thursday of this week is Christmas. Last Tuesday, the scholars' Christmas program at school was given for the families. The students had practiced very hard to make it a blessed Christmas. Everyone was able to attend without any sickness. It was indeed joyful to see how the scholars' characters were growing and building in their self-esteem. I also thought how meaningful it was on all levels for them.

Miss Lizzie Farmwald's memorization class gave full witness to the Christian education. The recitation I was told in sign sent a message about who Jesus is to any outsiders who do not attend bi-weekly church services. The classroom was attractively decorated and the atmosphere was very pleasant. This spoke well of our school. The scholars' work was exhibited in the classroom for the family viewing.

My class signed "Jesus Loves Me" and "Silent Night." I held up a Christmas poem written by eight-year-old Evonne Raber. She signed it beautifully as Miss Farmwald read it out loud for her peers, family, and friends.

Preparing a program of this magnitude gives both children and teachers a change of activity following the long hard pull of the first year together. This program and break gives us all a fresh start for the next few months ahead. The majority of hard work usually occurs during January, February, and March.

Rebekah, Deborah, Ruth, Leah, and I baked many pies for Christmas, along with cookies, fudge, and other candies.

Isaiah signed, "In some Districts, celebration of Christmas lasts two days. Christmas Day is reserved for fasting, meditations, Scripture reading, and other religious activities that focus on the celebration of the birth of Jesus Christ."

December 26 (or second Christmas) is meant for celebration with family and friends, with gift giving, gatherings, and feasting. This Christmas was my first with the Amish and totally different from any previous Christmases.

Isaiah signed, "No Amish District, no matter where, celebrates Santa Claus! Christmas cards may be sent to family and friends providing they are not extravagant. There are no decorations of trees with lights since no one has electricity in our District. We let our families string cards received around the room in our homes. Then the children open their gifts. In the afternoon, the Amish gather around for a big family meal. Since Christmas is on Thursday this year, we will have our usual Sunday church services at home. If Christmas had fallen near the end of the week, like Saturday, we would have had church on Christmas morning instead of Sunday regular service."

The meal we prepared was roasted turkey, mashed potatoes and gravy, stuffing, salad, fruits, bread, cakes, cookies, pies, candy, and lots of coffee and milk.

Isaiah signed, "In some Districts with large families, many celebrations continue well into February. Otherwise it would be impossible to go to all of the gatherings in two short days."

Due to the heavy snow, the children wanted to play outside. They had much fun going down hills on homemade sleds, ice skating, snowball fights, and building snowmen. Isaiah and I joined in and had just as much fun building them.

Since school will get out earlier than the non-Amish schools due to spring planting, we remain in school throughout part of the Christmas season. Isaiah signed, "The main focus of the season, as I earlier mentioned (numerous times), and not to be forgotten, is the celebration of our Savior's birth. Even though we spend much time devoted to prayer and Scripture, spending time with our families, relaxing, and laughter are equally important to the Amish culture."

Chapter 27

Ice Fishing

I received a beautiful Christmas card from Christine and Paul. They are still excited about Paul's movie career. He continues making movies and becoming well known. We, of course, don't go to movies, so I will not see him perform. They wished Joshua, Rebekah, Isaiah, and all of the family a blessed Christmas. We strung their card up with others we received. It was a wonderful Christmas and I was feeling a contentment that had once been foreign to me.

Countless family members came from all over the country to spend the week. With all of the coming and going to visit or receive visitors, I wasn't sure if I was "coming or going!" I would go to bed tired and wake up excited to see what the next day would bring. It was a joyous time for everyone!

Work never stopped, however. We were cooking, mending, or quilting for the women folk. The men folk also performed their daily chores. We had a lot of help with the work and enjoyed sweet fellowship and quality time together. I still had to teach all week, but it was exciting to have the children sign, telling about their families arriving from Pennsylvania, southern Indiana, Ohio, Michigan, and elsewhere. We had hymn signing on Sunday evening and oh how I wish I could have heard their voices!

I was always amazed when the horses and buggies arrived. The snow was so deep and sometimes the temperature would drop to zero or below. However, the horses and buggies managed to get through. Isaiah's family still continued to come, visit, and share their love for the birth of our Lord and Savior, Jesus Christ.

Tuesday was a monthly sewing day and we knotted 12 large comforters and six

crib-size quilts. One of the ladies, Emma, faithfully sits and binds them as we all work together. It is indeed a busy time right now, but everyone says this is slow. Come spring, we will be very busy! As I look out the window at the snowflakes coming down, I decide to enjoy the beauty of the season and let tomorrow take care of itself. I am where I want to be!

Christmas was behind us now and the month of January is also gone. February is really going slowly and we will be out of school in March. I have so much enjoyed being able to teach and watch my deaf class learn to speak a new language. This will be retained by them for the rest of their lives. Education is a two-way street, because I have learned a great deal during this process as well. Their families have learned to sign right along with them in the comfort of their homes at night. Many parents have written me letters, thanking me and letting me know how their lives have opened up a new world for them now that they can communicate. As I reflect back on my life, I can identify with all of their frustrations, as well as their hunger for knowledge.

Isaiah and his brothers have been ice fishing. I cannot believe anyone would want to make a hole in a frozen pond or lake and sit on a cold bucket and fish with only a lantern to keep them warm. They do this for many days and bring home a lot of fish for our meals, which are delicious once Rebekah fries them. I even learned how to scale them and prepare them for frying. Ah, the results are worth it! I remember Rebekah told me that the way to a man's heart is through his stomach.

Isaiah signed, "Maybe Saturday you can go with us and experience the fun of catching fish and watching my brothers ice skate across the pond."

"Maybe I will skate, too, if they teach me. You can catch our meal while I have fun learning how to skate!"

His smile assured me that he did not believe I could ice skate any easier than I could learn to ice fish.

When Saturday arrived, it was still very cold. Isaiah signed, "I will put plastic around your feet after you put your warm stockings on. You may want to wear your knitted slippers, too, before I put the plastic on your feet."

By the time he did all of that, I was unable to get my feet into my skates, but his brother, Jacob, had bigger boots I could wear to ice fish. Once again, I saw the smile on Isaiah's face as he set me up to ice fish, believing I wouldn't catch any.

The ice-fishing pole was really short and I found myself having to get up and walk backward slowly whenever I had a fish on the line because the pond was so deep. Then, of course, I would lose the fish back in the water. I did this numerous times until Isaiah saw me and showed me how to set the hook so I would not lose anymore.

When we left the pond to go home, I had 16 fish and Isaiah had 14. His family laughed with us as to who was the better fisherman.

Isaiah signed, "The next time you go to the pond, Collie, you can skate!"

We had hot chocolate and Rebekah had made cookies. Yummy! I was still very cold and sat close to the warm stove, reflecting as I often do since being here. Oh what fun we had today! I am already looking forward to the next time! I realize, as time progresses, I am becoming more attached to Isaiah and his family. It concerns me in one respect that Isaiah has never encouraged me in any way to be anything but his friend. His family, however, has made me feel like a daughter and a sister. I try not to think too much about Isaiah and a possible future with him as his wife. It can never happen, because his Amish upbringing allows him only to marry within his faith and culture. When I have these feelings, I pray God will redirect me to reflect back on my teaching and reveal my purpose for being here: to show the deaf people and the Amish community that the deaf can hear. They need to make time to speak to each other so they can read lips or learn to sign some of our language. This process helps me put Isaiah out of my mind for a while.

Chapter 28

Surprise Birthday

Isaiah is still teaching me Pennsylvania Dutch and he signed that I am a good student. I must admit it has begun to get a little easier.

One night I signed to Isaiah and Joshua, "Some of the parents believe our school problems are the fault of the teachers. I personally feel some of the fault lies with the parents, because they don't like the teachers insisting the students sign or talk in English at recess. Many of the students do not understand the English language well enough and, therefore, cannot comprehend what they read or what they sign. This process also enters into their studies such as arithmetic and English.

"Other parents want to save money on books and paying teachers. I think the biggest problem is parents keeping the students home to work for sometimes up to two weeks in succession. I understand that sometimes it is necessary to keep them home to work, but teaching a child who is not there is impossible. Sometimes we may not see a boy for up to three weeks due to farm work. Not only is it not legal, but the teachers do not like it either. What kind of example are the children being taught?"

Joshua told Isaiah to sign me a story. "A teacher had trouble teaching her class and maintaining control of her classroom. The

few rules she had were not enforced and the pupils had the run of
the school. Recesses were extended far beyond the time allowed.
She wanted the scholars to like her, so she granted them every
favor they asked. Instead of liking her, they called her disrespectful
names. Still, she granted more favors, hoping to win their love that
way.

"One day, one of the boys was too lazy to do his arithmetic, so
he went to her and asked for the answer book. She gave it to him
and from that day forward, her answer book was in the hands of
every scholar. After the scholars made copies of the answers and
got their work done, they stood up and walked around as they
pleased. She was finally replaced and the new teacher was very
strict. Perhaps this is why some parents kept their children home at
the beginning of the school year. Maybe they thought they would
learn more at home.

"I must tell you, Collie, you and Lizzie Farmwald are good
teachers and have the respect of parents and children alike. Continue
to do what you're doing. It is visible to all of us that you enjoy
teaching and you are visible to the scholars."

This encouragement I received from both of these learned men
has helped me, as a teacher, maintain the needed perseverance the
scholars have come to expect from me. As I prepared for school the
next day, I felt vibrant and of more value.

It has been a while since Isaiah and I made a trip into town.
He signed, "We need to visit some family members and see if
we can get some of them to go skating and ice fishing again this
weekend."

I signed in return, "I have caught a cold and want to stay at
home this weekend to rest."

He signed that he understood. Besides, it was February 16,
1994, my birthday. This day was greeted with heavy-falling snow
and frigid cold. I began wondering what this 37th birthday would
bring. I looked up and saw Deborah at my open door. She signed,
"Collie, Mem wants you to come downstairs."

I walked into the living quarters and Jeanna and Kevin were sitting there with their 10-month old son, Zachery. I began crying and they hugged me and signed, "Surprise! Happy birthday! Collie, it is not too far for us to come visit you by car."

All three of them looked well and I was so happy to see them. Rebekah had a birthday cake, coffee, and ice cream for the gathering they had planned. Even though the weather was frightful, all of Isaiah's brothers and sisters were there to celebrate. They gave me knitted gloves and a scarf. I had so many hugs and no one in the world felt more loved than I did this night!

Jeanna signed to me that the library I worked at in Fort Wayne had caught on fire. Many of the beloved books I handled with love and care were lost. No one was injured and they built a new library in the same spot within a year.

"It is modern and when you come to see us, we will make it a point to go there and browse. Donna is still the librarian and she sends you her love and best wishes for your life here. She is anxious to see you again!"

We visited for quite a while. It was late and time for them to return home. I was pleased that Kevin and Isaiah were enjoying each other's company.

After they had gone, Isaiah signed, "Were you surprised?"

I signed, "Pleasantly, thank you."

Isaiah commented in sign, "When you see them and their son, it gives me hope that someday I may have a son as well."

I fell asleep quickly that evening, but my dreams were full of Isaiah and me being in love, having a family, and living here in Amishland, where God provided me with a simple life and an abundance of love, like I have always wanted, for as long as I can remember. I was reminded how I used to think why can't anyone love me and why doesn't anyone hug me?

Reality arrived the next morning when I was awakened by knowing it was only a dream! I thanked God for His help in dealing with my loneliness, by providing me with such a loving family. I also thanked Him for the comfort His daily presence brings to me. I asked Him to help me reach out to others with compassion, trusting that I can help them to do well in their lives and in whatever way He uses me. That He will allow me to be a blessing in other's lives; because, I read in His Word, we are blessed to be a blessing. I felt much better after my prayer and eagerly got ready for whatever the day would bring.

Chapter 29

Acceptance

I spoke to God again last night and unburdened my heart to Him. My life has changed entirely since I first arrived in northeastern Indiana! I am reasonably content, my profession is quite satisfying, and Isaiah's family and the Amish way of life are very pleasing to me. I still dream of finding the happiness of a loving man who will be my husband and father to my children. It is not acceptable to me to be alone and I only want what Christine and Jeanna have – to be married, have children, love someone, and be loved in return. I specifically asked God to grant me my prayerful request if it is His will for me; or to accept that I will always be content with knowing how much He loves me. I selfishly added I hope His will for me will include Isaiah. I cannot imagine meeting anyone else I could be happier with. If God chooses someone else for Isaiah, I would accept it and be happy for him, as I know he has expressed his desire to have a son someday. I thanked God and gave Him the "I Love You" sign, knowing He would understand my sign.

The next morning, I awoke refreshed and ready to begin school. We are already half way through February and school will soon be over. We still have a great deal to accomplish before the school year is finished and I knew I would need strength beyond my own.

We always start the school day with prayer. What a difference it makes to invite God into the classroom! To thank Him for His love and for providing us with the minds to learn and to share what we know with others; to love Him first and foremost.

Reflecting on my life, and, by the grace of God, I know I have come a long way in my faith and realize how unique He has made each one of us. I see the uniqueness in each student and, especially, the deaf children I teach. The eagerness to learn is still in the classroom, but the restlessness strives to take over at the end of the day.

The hearing children are more restless. Miss Lizzie Farmwald handed me a note saying, "Collie how do you manage to control your classroom? The students look to you for direction and guidance. I see no unnecessary distractions with them as they await your instructions."

I signed back to her, "It should not be a classroom of death, but a classroom of life!"

She wrote back to me saying, "Most of the year, I have noticed your pupils have a hushed quietness, and not from just being hearing-impaired. They have quietness with their lessons and do not want to disturb their neighbors."

I said to her in the note, "This is almost the end of the school year and restlessness is common. Lizzie, remember, my scholars cannot hear or speak, so they are going to be naturally quiet. You are a good teacher as well! You help the children truly enjoy seeing new insights, hearing new sounds, thinking new thoughts, all the while making it interesting."

She smiled in return, and her demeanor changed while her pupils settled into the lesson she had prepared.

When Isaiah picked me up he signed, "Collie, you only have about two weeks of school left, are you anxious to get out?"

I signed, "I am and have thought about what this spring and summer will bring. Do you think I can spend time with Kevin and Jeanna?"

Isaiah signed in return, "Spring is a busy time for us, with a lot of planting and work to be done. How long would want to be away?"

"Right now, it is just a thought," I signed. "I will see what the next two weeks bring."

Upon arrival at Isaiah's house, Rebekah signed, "Shingles are going around again. I certainly hope we don't get them!" She indicated I had a letter from Jeanna and Kevin. I was excited to read what is happening to them.

Jeanna wrote that they would be gone most of the month of May, as Zachary is growing so quickly they want to take him on a vacation. That answered my question from Isaiah about visiting them in the spring. I was not really disappointed, as I could concentrate on helping Rebekah with finishing the garden and any other tasks she had planned.

We have been having a great deal of rain lately. Rebekah signed, "I plan to quilt tomorrow and, as it seems to always happen, it is very windy and rainy so we will enjoy working inside."

"Will you make shoofly pie for tomorrow?"

Laughing Rebekah signed, "You are becoming Amish my daughter, Collie." My eyes began to tear up as I thought what a wonderful compliment to be called Rebekah's daughter.

In response, I signed, in Pennsylvania Dutch, "You have many boblis (babies), yet you chose to leeva (love) me. You eah (honor) me, Maem (mother). I am dankboah (thankful)!"

Rebekah signed, "Isaiah has taught you our language well!"

The remaining two weeks of school passed by very quickly. It was now time to begin packing up my lessons and other paraphernalia in crates. The children helped me on the last day. After completing all of the tasks, we all went outside for the rest of the afternoon and played games and enjoyed ourselves. Isaiah came to get me and loaded all of the crates into the buggy. As we left for the summer, I thanked God for the school year we just completed and began looking forward to the spring and summer.

I could not believe another year had passed. Spring is here again! This week is displaying many signs of a long-awaited spring: some Marlins are back with their cheery chatter, tulips have begun to open up, daffodils are in full bloom, and early seeds have been planted. The other day, Isaiah's brother, Joseph, mowed the lawn after all the rain. The temperature is now climbing to the 70s. Oh, how I love spring!

On Good Friday, Isaiah's family all gathered around to celebrate. On Easter Sunday we had church at Anna Troyer's, who is one of my student's parents. Our visiting ministers were Bishop Ora Miller and Bishop Samuel Nolt from a neighboring District. The home church was full and Bishop Nolt ended the lengthy sermon from Hebrews 9:12: "By His own blood, He entered in once into the Holy place having obtained eternal redemption for us."

On Sunday evening, Anna Troyer's eldest sister had a singing for the young folks. Twenty-seven people came. We were also invited, and I enjoyed watching them. Anna and two of my other students, Levi Mast and Evonne Raber, signed to one another, as we lip read the words being sung. Isaiah filled us in on the words he was able to hear. We certainly had a wonderful day and evening!

I couldn't help looking back on my past and comparing when I lived with Steve, Karen, Bobby, and Rita with the present day. Then we hid Easter eggs, ate chocolate bunnies, and celebrated the day much differently. Now I feel more at peace being with the Amish, or plain people, and being less worldly. I have been accepted as never before, and am loved with a sense of belonging I have always craved and desired. I can now honestly say I have it all with this family!

Unfortunately, shingles appeared once again in the home. Joshua was the victim. He suffered with much itching and pain.

Chapter 30

The Year There Was No Summer

Rebekah was concerned and worried about Joshua and his shingles because of the spring work that was yet to be done. Isaiah assured Rebekah that with Amos, Jacob, Joseph, and him, they would get all of the work accomplished on time. He should just rest, get well, and let them take over. He will be able to help when he is well again, but, for now, the brothers are grown and old enough to pull their weight.

One evening, as Isaiah and I were alone together, he signed, "Collie, we are blessed with a warm and beautiful spring this year! My great-grandparents passed down a story about the year there was no summer during the mid–1800s in a New England state, because January or the first part of the winter was so dry and cold. From spring to early fall they experienced a series of cold waves that damaged major crops and greatly reduced the food supply."

"How did they live and what was the impact?"

"My grandmother kept a diary all year. In fact, most women kept diaries every year to compare planting, seeding, and other events to pass down to their families. In some areas of New England and the northeast, June experienced a widespread snowfall."

I signed, "That is hard to comprehend!"

"I know," Isaiah signed. "As a result of this snowfall, corn did not ripen and hay, fruits, and vegetables were greatly reduced in quantity and quality from Maine and Vermont, all the way south to New Jersey and beyond the East Coast. Vermont's weather in June felt like September – the wind was cold and piercing like early winter. Snow and hail fell!"

"In June? Oh, Isaiah, I never would have thought that could happen!"

"Grohs-mammi (grandmother) said people commented it was beyond anything they had ever known. Gloves, coats, and hats had to be worn until noon just to keep warm. Birds sought shelter in barns and houses, and many fell dead in the fields. In New Hampshire, frost killed the bean crop. In Maine in July, frost killed the beans, cucumbers, and squash."

I signed, "Not in July!"

"Yes, Collie, in July! Cold waves in August crossed New York and New England and corn again was destroyed. Connecticut lost their most important crop, Indian corn. It was so unripe, moldy, and soft that even the hogs and cattle couldn't be fattened! They couldn't even make cornmeal."

"Oh my," I signed. "Why did it happen?"

"Grohs-mammi thought some diaries mentioned it was because of a volcano eruption, but I don't think anyone really knows. Regardless, I do believe it is why the ancestors left New England and migrated to Indiana and Illinois. Our Old Order Amish belief is old-fashioned for a number of reasons, because it could happen again, maybe even here. Consequently, we have learned to limit our farming, thereby making it less risky with a smaller investment."

"Isaiah, you have signed to me the most interesting history lesson. I will use some of this from your Grohs-mammi, if it is okay with you to teach the children next year."

"Collie, you may teach whatever you choose. I am so happy I remembered to tell you of this time period! We are so blessed! This fine, warm, spring day has opened my heart with joy to be able to share and be with you."

As I retired to bed, I thanked God for my life here in Isaiah's home with all of his family. I asked God to please bring someone into my life – someone like Isaiah, who is kind and loves God and his family. "God," I prayed. "Isaiah is a hard worker and loves

the land. He accepts me and my handicap and has compassion for everyone. He loves as You love and gives of himself whole-heartedly in appreciation for what You have done for him." I ended my prayer with the sign, "I love you forever!"

As I got into bed, I reflected on the story Isaiah had signed to me. I could barely embrace the year there was no summer and attempted to picture his Grohs-mammi when the story was passed down. I must never take for granted how Isaiah and his family live, work, and surrender their hard work to receive abundant life from their land.

Isaiah, too, lay in his bed pondering my reaction to what his Grohs-mammi shared from her diary years before. He felt something was changing within me. His feelings were different now compared to how he felt a few weeks ago.

I need to sleep, as I will have a busy day tomorrow. Now is not the time to ponder such things!

Chapter 31

Shunning

Christine sent me a letter to inform me that she and Paul had gotten a divorce. I was hurt for her, yet I had to admit the last few letters I received made me question their marriage. Paul was extremely popular in Hollywood, California, thereby making Christine's disabilities all the more noticeable among his peers. Christine is so beautiful inside and out with outstanding Christian values. Apparently, Hollywood was not ready for honesty and goodness.

It seems Paul fell into a trap that Christine says happens all the time out there. She indicated she was going to stay out there for a while and try and use her talents to benefit her love for the theater and film. I pray for her, because she loved Paul so much. She expected their lives would remain together forever. I placed her letter aside and remembered how she believed that somewhere out in this great big world there was someone for me. I felt my confidence leaving and so wanted to believe her, then and now.

I asked God to help her through the heart-wrenching pain she must be feeling right now and bring joy back into her life. Maybe Christine will return to Indiana some day and find happiness once again. My concern for her was that after the blandness of living in Fort Wayne, she may not want to leave California, even if she remained alone forever.

In prayer, I said, "God, there are many forms of shunning. Handicapped people are aware of avoidance more than non-handicapped. Lord, please see that Christine finds a fellowship of believers who will support and comfort her." I felt immediate peace that God will take care of her as He always has.

Joshua finally got over the shingles. He is back in the fields and Rebekah and I have been very busy with the garden. The weeds are beginning to threaten to take over everything! With the whole family working so hard, we had little time for an outing.

Isaiah signed to me, "Collie, our family is going to Ivan Winger's. He lives north of here a short distance. The purpose is to watch him and his family make maple syrup. You will enjoy watching the process of syrup making."

I signed, "I am happy to go with you. Will we be able to eat some of it?"

Smiling, Isaiah signed, "We will bring some home my sheveshtah (sister). You will eat it, I assure you." I hoped Isaiah didn't see my startled expression. Sister is not what I want him to call me! He didn't appear to notice the return look I gave him.

"We will take the wagon so we can all go together into the woods where the maple trees are located."

Isaiah's brother, Amos, drove the horses and wagon and Isaiah signed to me what I was about to see.

"In the spring, the sugar water that was stored all winter runs and travels to the maple tree branches. This provides food for the leaves when they begin to grow. The sugar is the food for the growing tree. In God's creation of the land and trees, He provides this sweet sugar water to become sap. I will not try to go through the whole processing procedure with you, Collie, but as you observe the processing and have questions, feel free to get my attention and I will explain more. I will tell you that predicting the precise conditions needed to collect enough high-quality sap is a definite challenge. It differs all over the country as to when the sap comes in. It takes approximately 30-40 gallons of sap to make one gallon of syrup."

I signed back to him, "I see men drilling at various heights on the tree, what is the reason for that?"

"The various heights make it easier and more convenient to collect."

I signed, "What is that tube-like thing he puts in after he drills the hole?"

Isaiah explained, "It is called a spike. He will tap that into the drilled hole. It will carry the sap from the tree to the bucket."

I became so fascinated with the sap flowing that I could not sign anymore. I just wanted to enjoy the time we were spending in the woods. We went from procedure to procedure, then, finally, to the cooking process over the open fires. At the end of the collection process and the making of the syrup, we tasted the delicious flavor. True to his word, Isaiah and Joshua purchased some syrup.

The next morning, Rebekah made pancakes and they were delightful with fresh maple syrup.

Isaiah signed, "Collie, we are having a lot of showers this week. With the gravel and sandy soil, it is sorely needed! This will help our crops grow. The fruit trees and berries are blooming, the ones that were under row covers. We are already enjoying the dandelion greens fixed with bacon. Rhubarb will be ripe before long, as well. Can you feel the warmth of the soil under your feet?"

I signed, "Yes and how I love it!"

Isaiah signed, "Jacob and Joseph went mushroom hunting today. They brought back some black ones. In a couple of weeks, the yellow morels will be up and available. We will feast on them. Usually the woods behind the plowed and planted fields are plentiful. They are so delicious!

"Daed, Amos, Jacob, Joseph, and I have been so busy in the fields. We planted oats for the horses and cows. In about June or July, there will be plenty of food for the animals. Corn and soybeans planted at the same time will be harvested and used by our family and for selling. Some of the corn will be made into silage and placed in the silos. We like to have it all in by April 15. Another advantage of the Amish farmer is that our horses and plows get through the fields easier. We have seen tractors buried in the fields and they can't get them out until the rains cease."

I watched the men bring in a lot of cut wood for the cook stoves and winter heating. It seems like work is always ready for us whenever we have any free time. Summers go quickly and wood will be cut and stacked throughout this time.

Isaiah and I went on a buggy ride the other day and watched a local man climb up a windmill. He removed the windmill head with ropes, repaired it, painted it, and put it back up.

Isaiah signed, "A large percentage of us now have gas engines with conversion pumps that pump out the water from the ground through a pipe."

I find and notice that everything Isaiah shares with me is interesting and useful in my teaching. Everything is now in bloom and we have purple Martins and many Martin houses. Oh how I love spring!

Another letter from Christine arrived today and she appears happier. I am so delighted for her! Maybe God has answered my prayers.

"To my dear friend Collie: Oh, Collie! I met someone on the studio set. I am making a film about struggles, love, disappointments, and excitement in relationships. It is called *Following Your Dreams*. I am not the leading lady, but I have a good part. The man I met is Peter Marcus, and he has been acting in movies for a few years. I find him not only attractive, but comfortable to be with. I am going to proceed slowly because I am vulnerable right now and can easily get hurt again. I will write to you more frequently now that I have more time to myself. I don't see Paul anymore, but all of the gossip columns show him with someone different on each occasion. We are now in totally different circles. It appears Hollywood is known for unstable marriages and divorce is common. Are you and Isaiah getting anywhere in some type of a relationship? Have you let him know your feelings for him? Are you still so happy being with him and his family and living the Old Amish way of life? Write me and tell me what all of your days and nights are like in Indiana. I do miss you and Fort Wayne so much.

"You do understand why I cannot return yet, as I need to pursue my dream of becoming famous. Then we can return to the movie theater that kicked us out! Oh what fun we had that day! Do you remember? Sometimes I think we were just silly, young girls, but I still want to go back there. Maybe we will get kicked out again, no matter how big a star I become! Oh what lovely memories we shared together! I love you, Collie, and remember our 'love always' sign. Blessings to you all! Christine."

After I completed my work for the day, I sat down in my room and answered Christine's letter.

"Dear Christine, it is now late spring in Indiana. Work for all of us is ongoing. Planting, gardening, harvesting hay in the field, and, in general, working from dawn until dusk. But we will all reap the benefits of the hard work, so it is worth every hour of labor!

"Due to the long days, Isaiah and I don't see much of each other right now, so to answer your questions regarding our relationship, he does not have one inkling of my feelings for him. No, I have never told him how I feel! Sometimes I want to pour my heart out to him, but realize how absurd that would be if he does not feel the same about me. It is a hair-brained idea and I will not continue to expand upon it. A couple of years have gone by and we are not getting any younger, are we?

"I am so pleased for you and Peter. You deserve so many blessings. I am sorry you and Paul were unable to remain together. We both know, however, that God has a plan for our lives in His well-timed manner. Eventually, we will be made aware of His desires and what His plans for us will bring.

"I also remember the movie theater where we were kicked out. Someday we will return! I look forward to your being successful as an actress and our grand entrance into that old theater together. It is against my Old Amish Order beliefs to watch TV or go to theaters. However, maybe they will make an exception. It is unlikely, though, so don't be disappointed if I cannot attend. I will only mention it after the time comes for us to go and you have reached your dream. I do love and pray for you my special friend. Yes, I use the 'I Love You' sign more than you can imagine. The scholars at my school also love to use it with their families and friends. Take care of yourself and may God's blessings continue to be upon you, Christine. Love in Christ, Collie."

I slept soundly and awoke refreshed and ready for another busy day. We had an old-fashioned, hard thunderstorm during the night, bringing around two inches of rain.

Chapter 32

Rachel Arrives

Due to the heavy rain in the night, the fields are thoroughly soaked, so the men will not be able to work them today. Isaiah and I signed that we may make a trip to Shipshewana since we have the time. I signed, "Good! I want to mail a letter to Christine."

Sometime later, family friends arrived from Colon, Michigan: Levi and Ruth Parker, their daughter, Rachel, and son, John. Joshua and Rebekah were pleased! We prepared food for everyone and sat around and visited. I could read their lips and observed their love for one another. The most disconcerting part of the visit for me was watching Isaiah and Rachel interact. It was obvious she was smitten with him and he was flattered with her. I was hurt he introduced me as his sister. I didn't want to be rude, yet I didn't want to watch them together.

In sign, I excused myself to Rebekah and went to my room. This was the first time I saw Isaiah show any attention or interest in anyone since my arrival years before. It was unexpected, and I found myself fidgety, anxious, and uncomfortable being in the same room with them. I spotted Christine's letter and tore it up! How could I send it now after sharing my heart with her regarding Isaiah? I will write to her when I am less agitated. I must make myself go back downstairs and be kind to

Rebekah's family and friends. I have to remind myself I am a guest in their home as well and have much to be thankful for.

Isaiah and Rachel were still engaged in conversation, so I joined Rebekah and Ruth at the table. We had pie and coffee. Rebekah signed to me that the Parker family live in Colon, Michigan, but were considering moving to LaGrange County to be closer to us. I tried not to show my disappointment and smiled at Ruth. She could not sign, so Rebekah had a piece of paper and pencil on the table for us to use.

Later that night, when I retired, I asked God, "Will I ever find anyone Lord? Am I destined to spend my life never having a husband or children? Do I ask too much from you my Lord? You know the desires of my heart. Give me a sign, please! I am desperately trying not to feel sorry for myself."

Despite my despair over Isaiah's attention to Rachel, I slept well. Upon awakening, I came downstairs to begin the morning chores. Isaiah and his brothers were already in the fields and Rebekah, Ruth, and Deborah were preparing a wonderful breakfast.

While everyone was awakening, Rachel came down the stairs asking what she could do to help. Rebekah sent both of us out to gather eggs. We were quiet at first, and then slowly began to write back and forth. She wrote asking about my deafness and I wrote asking a lot of questions about her life in Colon. I did not want to like her yet, but I did. She was quite attractive, with blond hair, blue eyes, and a smile that let you know you were special. I could see immediately why Isaiah would want to be with her! She wrote that she was 21 years old, the same age as Isaiah's brother, Amos. I wrote that Isaiah and I were both in our late 30s. She wrote that she knew Isaiah was older, but he was the sweetest man anyone could ever hope to know. I had to agree with her, even though I could see her interest in him was not the same as it was for Amos, or even Jacob, who was 19 now.

When we returned to the house, the men had arrived for breakfast. Once again, Isaiah and Rachel sat beside one another and talked the whole time he was eating. Isaiah barely looked at me, as he seemed to be so taken by her. Rebekah signed to me that she, Ruth, Rachel, and I will do the shopping, while Deborah, young Ruth, and Leah will do the dishes and clean the house. Once again, I realized I was the only non-vocal person among the four of us.

In her wisdom, Rebekah had me sit beside her in the buggy on the way to Shipshewana to shop. In sign, she kept me up to speed with the conversation taking place. It is early June and the trip was beautiful. Everything was in bloom and it was so sunny and warm. If my spirit could be higher and I was with Isaiah, it would be a perfect day. I need to stop thinking this way. I need to acknowledge what I see happening between Isaiah and Rachel and decide what I intend to do with my future. First, I must give it some time to see what I believe is developing between the two of them.

As we approached Shipshewana, we noticed there had been a shop fire at John and Erma Millers and the building was completely destroyed. Rebekah stopped and we walked over to Erma. She shared with us that the fire may have started with a generator. John's trade is carpentry and they will rebuild, of course. Most of the time I was able to lip read what she was saying, but Rebekah explained more as we continued on to Shipshewana.

Shopping was busy today, with many visitors in town who want to watch all of us in our dress and see what we are buying. I will never get used to the fact that many people come here just to see the Amish and the culture of the plain folk. We often have to lower our heads and turn away when we see a camera come out of nowhere. I know it is difficult for them to understand our not wanting to be photographed and remember when Isaiah explained this to me.

With shopping completed, we arrived home. Deborah and Leah did a wonderful job of cleaning! By the time we put away our groceries, it was time to prepare supper. The men folk came in and we washed up and proceeded to sit down and eat.

I could lip read some of Isaiah's and Rachel's conversation, but I didn't want to appear nosey. So I signed to Deborah about the animals. In sign she told me about six new kittens that were born and asked if I wanted to see them after the supper dishes were done. I then saw Isaiah sign to Rachel about the same kittens and asked if she wanted to see them later. She smiled readily and agreed to go. They were the cutest baby kittens, all black and white. I particularly liked a black one with a white ring or circle around his eye. He also had a white paw.

I signed to Isaiah, "May I please keep this kitten for my own?"

"Rachel expressed a desire in that particular one, as well, to take to their new home when they find one, but you can enjoy it for the remaining time it is here."

I signed, "I will select another so I don't become too attached to this one, thank you."

Rachel had no idea what we discussed and continued to smile and gently pet the kitten I wanted. This was okay with me, as my second choice was mostly white with a black-tipped tail. It had black all around his left ear and he seemed to fit me well. I decided to name him "Lokka," which is Pennsylvania Dutch for "to call an animal." Plus, I just like the name Lokka!

This morning we all went to church at Samuel Kutz's house. The first time Levi, Ruth, and Rachel went to church with us was at Floyd and Mary Yoder's house. There may have been 30 or 40 people attending church and most everyone commented on what a beautiful singing voice Rachel has.

Isaiah signed, "I wish you could hear her sing, because you would love the wonderful, soft voice she has."

"Someday I will, Isaiah. I will not always be a deaf mute. God will heal me, only maybe not this side of heaven."

He smiled that endearing smile that has captured my heart over and over for several years and signed, "You are a good woman, Collie, and I am pleased for your friendship."

The food after church is always so good! All of the fresh garden foods – beans, broccoli, cucumbers, beets, cabbage – and many other wonderful foods are served. Rebekah signed, "I saw my first ripe, red tomato today."

Someone mentioned there was a house close by that may become available for the Parker family. Deborah signed, "It is not far from where we live and it is in our church District."

She signed to me," I know Isaiah is spending a lot of time with Rachel. I do believe Amos likes her, also. I watch how he looks at her and it is difficult for everyone concerned when both brothers show the same interest."

My reply in sign to her was, "Rachel is young, beautiful, warm, and friendly. I can certainly understand why many men are fascinated with her!"

Deborah gave me a big hug and signed, "You have all the same qualities, Collie."

I haven't looked in a mirror for years, but I knew I was not easy to look at, let alone beautiful. However, I was pleased Deborah attempted to make me feel better.

Rebekah asked me to walk with her this afternoon. She is concerned about my reaction to Isaiah and Rachel being together so much.

I signed, "I miss the time Isaiah and I spent together. He taught me so much concerning the Old Amish traditions and explaining his thoughts and feelings about everyone he loves. He is a good man and I want him to find happiness, even if it means without my involvement in his life. I will support any choices he makes regarding his future. I already know he will always see me as his sister."

Rebekah signed, "Rachel was a very young girl, in her early teens, when Isaiah and all of us saw her last. She was always fascinated with Isaiah, and no one knows what will happen now that they are moving here from Michigan. I hope you and Rachel will be friends. Eventually, she will learn to sign and then you and she will better communicate."

I thanked Rebekah for walking and sharing her thoughts with me. She is such a wonderful maem (mother).

I knew I would need time before I could be Rachel's friend. I admitted to myself that I am in love with Isaiah and it is difficult watching them together. My hopes and dreams for a future for us are waning and it is going to be difficult to stay here.

"Dear Christine," I wrote. "I am unable to explain everything to you in this letter, as I am having a difficult time right now. I would like to come to California to see you and meet Peter. If possible, I would like to stay for a while if that's okay. The sooner the better actually! I have saved some money from my years of teaching. I have never flown before and am quite concerned about it, but please let me know if this is a convenient time for you. If not, I understand perfectly. I miss you, my friend, and look forward to hearing from you. Love in Christ, Collie."

I went downstairs and signed to Rebekah that I needed to go into town. She signed, "Deborah will take you after lunch and dishes are done. She needs to buy some sewing items I will need."

She gave me a big hug. Every loving response from her or any family member is a cherished moment. It will be hard to let go of them if and when I go to Christine's.

A week has passed and I have not heard from Christine. It is probably a little too soon to expect mail to get to California and return. It may take a bit longer than I thought.

Chapter 33

The Airplane Ticket

Thirteen-year-old Leah came running into the garden yelling. I watched her face and knew she was happy and excited! Everyone got up and ran to the barn. I followed and saw why everyone was elated. Candy, their filly, had given birth to a beautiful colt, with the assistance of Joshua and Isaiah. It was such a beautiful brown colt with a white diamond on its forehead.

I watched in awe as the colt tried to stand on his spindly legs. But, when he did, he was the most beautiful sight I had ever seen! The whole family celebrated with hugs for one another. Isaiah grabbed Rachel's hand and brought her closer to see the colt. Then I noticed the expression on Amos' face. It was clear to me he was not just taken by Rachel, he was in love with her! I could identify the turmoil that resided within him. My, how our lives have changed since the Parkers arrived from Colon, Michigan! How will Amos and I cope with our feelings?

I received a letter from Christine today. Not only is she excited I want to spend time with her, she even sent me an airline ticket to come to California in less than a week. My mind was racing as I read her letter. Oh my! How will I ever get to the airport? What airport do I use? What will I take with me? I have worn only Amish clothes for years.

What will Joshua and Rebekah say? Will they shun me from now on? What will Isaiah say and will he miss me? What do I need to do first?

I paced the bedroom with all of these thoughts whirling through my head. I picked up the letter again and Christine wrote, "Collie, not only will you be able to stay with me, but you will see other deaf people who work with actresses and actors. I am so excited to see you again! A schedule is enclosed. If you need help at the airport, just remember to have your pad of paper and pen with you. I hope I gave you enough time to get packed and make arrangements. I love you, Collie, and look forward to seeing you! Love, Christine."

The departure date on the ticket was late Friday afternoon. This being Tuesday already, I must not prolong informing Isaiah and his family of the plans I have made. They will help me with arrangements, I am sure. Maybe Isaiah will miss me a little, too. When I came in from the porch after reading my letter, I saw Rebekah and Ruth in conversation.

Rebekah looked at me and in sign said, "Collie, you look like you have lost your best friend, are you all right?"

In sign, I asked, "Can we go somewhere, so I can explain everything to you?"

We went toward the cornfield and I signed, "I have written Christine asking if I could go visit her. She answered me already and has sent a plane ticket with her response. She would like me to leave on Friday this week. I am concerned about getting transportation to the nearest airport. Do you think you can help me?"

Clearly Rebekah was surprised. She signed, "Are you sure you want to go? How long will you be gone? Yes, I will see that you get to the airport on time. Oh, Collie, I will be so sad to see you leave. I will speak with Joshua and the family tonight and we will make all of the arrangements. Have you told Isaiah?"

"No, I only received the letter today and did not expect an airplane ticket to be with the letter."

I didn't see Isaiah until the following morning. He signed, "Let's take a walk. Collie, I cannot imagine you flying to California for an unlimited period of time. I knew you wanted to see Christine for a while. Maem made it sound like you may be gone for a long time. What about teaching this winter?"

"The best answer I can give is, 'I do not know how long I will stay.' The question is, 'Do I have a place here in which to return, or will I be shunned like others?'"

"You will not be shunned as others, for you have not been baptized yet into our church with all of our beliefs and traditions. Collie, was this a sudden decision for you, or have you wanted to go on a more permanent basis for a while?"

"Isaiah, I have been confused lately and believe this decision is the best for me right now. I will miss you all so much and want you to know that I appreciate all you have done for me, taught me, and shared with me. You will always be very dear to me and a wonderful friend." Even now I am unable to share my real, heartfelt, honest feelings for him.

Isaiah signed, "This sounds like you have thought it through very well, but it sounds very permanent to me."

I signed, "Do you know what arrangements have been made for me on Friday? Today is already Wednesday and I am concerned about getting to the right airport for my plane."

"Collie," Isaiah signed, "The reason I wanted to take this walk with you was to find out about your plans. I just wanted to make sure this is really what you want to do. Do you remember Bill, the driver who brought you here from Fort Wayne?"

"Yes," I signed. "He is a very nice man."

"He will pick you up here on Friday. As indicated on your flight itinerary, you are flying from Fort Wayne nonstop to Los Angeles, California. Christine is expecting you and will be waiting at the airport. Collie, are you sure this is what you want to do? It will change your life so much and take you away from all of us who love you. I want you to be happy, but I will miss you."

"I have much to do before Friday and must go back inside to begin getting my personal things in order."

I turned and left Isaiah standing with a bewildered look on his face. I contained my tears until I got to my room and then, like a fountain, the tears flowed. I cried into my pillow until I fell asleep. The next morning, I cleaned myself up and made my bed. I placed some personal things into the bag I used when I first came here. When I went down to breakfast the men were already in the fields.

Rebekah, Ruth, Rachel, and I had coffee together. I had trouble eating as I was so nervous. "Can you believe tomorrow is the day I leave?" I signed to Rebekah. "Will anyone be going to the airport with Bill and me?"

She explained, "Deborah and I will be going along. In case you need to stop or need anything, Bill cannot read sign, so we want to make sure you get on the right airplane and will be okay!"

I thanked her for everything, but had a huge lump in my throat and went outside to walk around and clear my mind.

I saw the colt and laughed at Lokka my cat. I will miss the farm and all of the animals, as well as this wonderful family. I have spent many years of my life here and a new start is frightening. I asked the Lord to bless this family that took me in, loved me, and made me a part of their lives. I will always be indebted to them! I prayed for Isaiah to find happiness and that he and Rachel will love one another. I prayed He will fill their lives with His blessings and Word.

After my prayer, I saw Rachel approaching me with a paper and pen in hand wearing her beautiful smile. We sat on the ground next to the barn and she wrote to me, "Collie, I have enjoyed meeting you. I wish I could speak your language and use my hands in the beautiful way I have seen you do, when you sign."

I wrote back thanking her and asked if her family had yet found a farm to purchase. She wrote that they were definitely interested in one nearby. She continued to write that she would miss me. I, in turn, wrote that I hoped she would find happiness here.

We sat in silence for a while and then got up to return to the house. We hugged and she waited for me to walk away. I saw Isaiah approaching and he walked directly to her and stood at her side. I felt his overwhelming presence as I left them together and knew I had made the right decision to leave the next day.

Early the next morning, after chores, I went upstairs to finish my packing. I placed my savings in a satchel I carry all of the time when

I go shopping. I then made sure the bedroom was immaculate. It was almost lunch time. I kept waiting for the men folk to come in from the field, but Deborah signed that Leah was taking their lunch to them so they can eat and get right back to work.

I was disappointed, but maybe it's easier for all to say goodbye, including me. I went downstairs and waited for Bill. When he arrived, he ate lunch and talked to all of the women. He has a particular interest in Rachel, too. She smiled sweetly at him and they were all laughing at something someone said.

Chapter 34

Leaving

As we left the farm, I looked in the field. There I saw Isaiah with the horses. He never glanced our way as I looked back at the road that was taking me far away from the home in which I had come to love and feel secure. Even more important, I was being taken away from the only man I have ever truly loved! My heart felt heavy, and, silently, I once again asked God, "Be with me my Lord in this new adventure in my life. Keep me safe and help my breaking heart to heal. Please keep Isaiah and his family safe as well." We arrived at the airport. There were so many airplanes! I was not sure which one was mine. Bill spoke to Rebekah as he guided us to the right one. We arrived early, but I didn't mind, as I loved to watch the airplanes fly in and out.

Deborah was excited and signed, "Oh, Collie, I wish I could go with you! I love you and will miss you so much."

I urged her to use her gift of sign this summer to help the students and other family members use the language among themselves. "I especially want you to do that because Isaiah will forget if he does not use it frequently."

She signed, "I will, Collie. Your language is beautiful. Thank you for teaching it to us!"

As I got ready to board the plane, Rebekah handed me a stack of letters from each family member to read. She signed, "These are to read on your long journey west." I cried and so did she and Deborah. My sense of loss overcame my fear of flying for the first time.

Once I got into the beautiful sky, I was fine. I really was scared prior to getting up there, but quickly enjoyed it.

A man sitting next to me tried to visit with me. I smiled and read his lips. I brought out my pen and paper and wrote to him that I am a deaf mute, but we can communicate this way. He seemed okay with that and told me I was the most pleasant deaf mute he had ever met! He went on to say he is a minister in California and proceeded to ask me on paper if I knew Jesus Christ as my Lord and Savior. I smiled and nodded yes. I wrote to him that in my faith we call ministers Bishops. We discussed the Old Order Amish until my hands got tired from writing. I was sure his were tired as well!

He wrote his name is Pastor Jack Webb and his church is St. Paul Lutheran in Hollywood. It is a relatively small church with a membership of approximately 350. He appeared fascinated when I wrote about our church services being conducted in one another's homes every other Sunday.

We both fell silent for a while and I turned to the letters I received from Isaiah's family. I had a letter from everyone but Joshua and Isaiah. I was disappointed in not receiving one from Isaiah, but Rebekah wrote for both she and Joshua. I read hers first.

"Dear Collette, it seems unapproachable for me to use your given name after calling you Collie for so many years. Yet, I love the sound of Collette, so I am using it in this letter. You are most assuredly not unapproachable, nor have you ever been. Your time with us has been too short! I have come to love you like a daughter. I want you to know you will always have a home with us. Joshua and I spoke this afternoon before you left and he feels the same way – that you're our child. God be with you! Submit all of your concerns to Him. Stay in His Word, for you will be challenged every day. Remember Romans 12:2: 'Be not conformed to this world.' You have our address, so please write often. We will be praying for you. Love, Joshua and Rebekah."

I felt such heaviness in my heart! I closed my eyes and once again thanked God for this family who loves me unconditionally. I looked over at Pastor Webb and he had a contented expression on his face. I tried to sleep, only to feel the vibration of the airplane engines roaring beneath me. I looked around at other passengers and they were looking out the windows, as though lost in their thoughts. I began to contemplate what I would be doing in California and the excitement of being with Christine once again.

I picked the letter from Deborah to read next. "Your absence is already making our house feel empty. I miss you already. I mentioned this feeling to Isaiah last night and he just walked away from me. What is wrong with him? He will barely talk to anyone. Even Rachel is staying away from him. Maybe he is just simply tired. All of the men have been really busy in the fields. If you do not get too busy, please write and tell me what you are doing. Until I see you again. Love, Deborah."

Pastor Webb woke up when the stewardess asked if we wanted anything to drink. He pointed to a coffee cup. I joined him and pointed to one as well. I gave him the sign for thank you.

He smiled again and wrote, "If that means thank you then you're welcome. Is there anything you need? If you need to use the restroom, I will ask the stewardess to show you where it is located."

Again I nodded and wrote, "Yes, that would be appreciated."

When she returned to pick up our cups, he told her I needed help. I followed her to the back of the plane and went into the smallest room I have ever seen. It was so small that I couldn't wait to open the door to have fresh air and space to move around. Another woman was waiting for me to come out and with pleasure I gave up the small room. I didn't drink anything else for the rest of the flight. I didn't eat anything, either, as I didn't want to go back in that closet of a room!

I opened another letter from Isaiah's younger sister Ruth. She signs very well, too. She and Leah helped me teach other children to sign. They caught on quickly and within six to eight months they signed frequently.

"Dear Collie," Ruth wrote, "everyone is sorry you're not here for church. The other children love you. You are a kind person and patient with us all. I am sorry you had to leave. We hope you will not stay away for very long. I love and miss you already. Love, Ruth."

I decided to read Leah's letter next.

"Dear Collie, I know you love it here. Why did you have to move away to California? Christine liked to come here to visit you because she liked the way we lived. Maybe she can come back to Indiana and live with us, too, or maybe she can live closer to us so we can still have you. Maybe you can think about all of this while you're away and will return home to be with us again. I love you forever, Leah."

I took a nap finally and woke up feeling refreshed.

Pastor Webb said we are about two hours away from Los Angeles. I stood up and stretched a little, thankful I did not have to use the bathroom. I asked Pastor Webb in a note if he would provide me with some insight into something I learned about faith at my Amish church.

I wrote, "In Romans 10:17, it says, 'Faith comes by hearing and hearing by the Word of God.' Then in Hebrews 11:6 it says, 'Without faith, it is impossible to please Him.' According to that, I cannot hear so I cannot have faith; and I cannot please Him without faith. How can I understand this when I am a deaf mute?"

Pastor Webb took my hand and smiled at me. He wrote on my pad, "Collie, you have great faith. I have only been with you for three or four hours and can already see the faith inside of you. You may not hear God's Word, but you read it and store it inside. You said a man in your family signs to you what the Bishop preaches in your home church. This man hears the Word and in turn gives it to you. God has used this man to be your ears. You please God by your prayers and love for others, but mostly for Him. You must not be concerned that you are not pleasing to God. Someday, when you go to heaven, you will hear every word spoken, every song sung, because you believe!"

I sat beside Pastor Webb absorbing what he wrote to me. I thanked him again and told him I was pleased we were seated beside one another.

Pastor Webb also wrote that God had a plan; and in that plan was our meeting each other, sitting together, and sharing our love for the

Lord and Savior. He also thanked me for sharing my Amish beliefs with him.

I returned to my letters. Both Joseph's and Jacob's read about the same. They will miss me and hope I find happiness in California with Christine. I decided to keep the letters from Amos and Rachel until I got settled and could read them on a day when I feel the need for my family's presence.

Pastor Webb wrote that the airplane pilot will come on the speaker and tell us when to fasten our seat belts.

"Above you, Collie, toward the front of the plane, you will see a monitor and it will say, 'Fasten seat belts!'"

I saw it light up and he wrote that we will soon descend and land at LAX. "After landing, I will help you find your friend. I hope to see you again someday!"

I smiled and thanked him once again.

We began deboarding and I spotted Christine and a handsome man with her. Pastor Webb was at my side and saw me wave. He shook my hand and I smiled at him, then he turned and walked away. I hoped I would get to see him again one day.

Christine introduced me to Peter and he gave me a hug. I felt genuine warmth from him. We retrieved my one suitcase from the baggage claim area, as I had my carry-on with me. We rode back to Christine's apartment with our hands flying back and forth. Peter continued to smile at me. I was in awe of all of the lights. The night brightness was so glaring because I had just come from a land of lanterns and, at times, total darkness.

Christine's apartment is beautiful! She has two bedrooms and a large bath. Her kitchen is really modern and nice and her living room is decorated beautifully.

"Collie," she signed. "This apartment is just one block from the studio, where I work. As you know, I cannot drive, so we will walk everywhere and have so much fun together."

Without telling me directly that my clothes were definitely out of place in the city, she signed, "We will go shopping for you tomorrow."

I signed in return, "We must keep these clothes in the closet, as they are a reminder of my previous, wonderful, happy life."

I began to cry. She wrapped her arms around me and let me cry my heart out. Peter left to return to his apartment so we could visit alone. He said he had an early day at the studio tomorrow.

Chapter 35

Overwhelming

I was exhausted, so we decided to retire early. Christine signed, "Sleep as long as you need, Collie, because I have Saturday through Wednesday off work so we can visit, shop for clothes, and simply get reacquainted again."

I thanked God for my safe arrival. I found it hard to believe that just this afternoon, I was in Shipshewana, Indiana, and tonight I am in Los Angeles, California. Christine reminded me that we are actually in Hollywood, California. I prayed for Pastor Jack Webb and his church and family. I prayed for Joshua and Rebekah and all of their family. I said a special prayer for Isaiah.

The next morning, Christine and I enjoyed a wonderful breakfast and coffee on her outdoor patio. It was already 76 degrees and the sun was bright and warm. It was so beautiful!

Christine signed, "Did you sleep well, Collie?"

"Not really," I signed. "I am not accustomed to such bright lights and could see an array of traffic lights outside my window. The countryside in Indiana is so dark, so it will take time for me to adjust to this world. I am used to using a lantern at night as opposed to turning on a light switch. I'm also used to doing chores in the morning with the animal smells in the barn. I'm in the modern world once again and have been out of touch for quite some time. I must admit, I miss the horses and buggies and the plain, simple life I have come to love! It is genuine hard work, Christine, but I learned to love the simple, uncomplicated, down-to-earth part of it all. When I feel the time is right and I am ready, we will have a discussion about Isaiah. Right now, I only want to enjoy you, the sun, the food, and the newness of this different world!"

"It has been such a long time," Christine signed. "I hope you will like Peter. He is a man of many talents. Hollywood will reward him because of them!"

"I like him already, Christine. He is an honest-to-goodness good hugger! I mean that in the most respectful way. Paul, on the other hand, was not as warm towards me."

She signed, "He was all about his career toward the end of our marriage."

I signed, "I am sorry to hear that, as you were so in love with him!"

"He is quite a big star now, Collie. He lacks for nothing financially and has his choice of women to satisfy his desires. He is still a good man down deep; he just got caught up with the fame, women, and money and had no room for me anymore. Peter, on the other hand, is a Christian, which is rare in this city and the profession we're in. We are cautious in our relationship. I do not want to suggest that our relationship will be perfect, for no one has perfection in their relationship. We will make decisions jointly on our love, God's love, and respect for one another. Not all marriage-minded people marry, Collie. Some of the noblest Christians have never been married."

Christine signed again, "Do you think Isaiah will ever marry?"

I signed, "I really don't know. My heart tells me he is who I want to marry, but he sees me only as a sister. Maybe he is one of those noble Christian men who will never marry. I am still unable to sort out my sadness of being away from him. In time, I will be able to share with you what I am feeling."

"Collie, we have a lot of time, so let's get ready and go shopping. I'll get my neighbor lady, who offered to drive us to the West Hollywood shopping area. She will pick us up around 4:00 and bring us back here when we are finished."

Sue, Christine's neighbor, arrived promptly and I was utterly amazed at the amount of vehicles zooming around us. It was a little scary!

After Sue dropped us off, I could not believe the people who were shopping! The stores were amazing! Restaurants and too many clothing stores to mention were available for whatever anyone desired. Christine was completely comfortable with this environment and I was shocked. I must have been a sight, because people starred at me in my mid-calf-length dress with black shoes. This simple style of dress in West Hollywood was definitely non-conforming to this part of the world. My Old Amish life was not a part of this world, and I wasn't interested in becoming a part of this world again. I truly love the neat, plain, simple, and serviceable clothes I have. How will I explain this to Christine?

We looked at clothes and I consistently nodded no.

Christine signed, "Collie, you do not have to conform to the lifestyle here, but you may want to try and wear something that will allow you to fit in a little better with the people and not draw attention to yourself."

We went to at least four more stores. I purchased a blouse, simple scarf, and a skirt that came almost to my calf. It was straight, not full, gathered, or pleated. We then went to a shoe store. A lady walked out wearing the highest heels I have ever seen. I turned to walk away when Christine grabbed my arm, pulled me back into the store, and smiled at me. I tried on several pair she picked out and kept signing, "No, no, no!"

Finally, I spotted a pair on the shelf. They were not my basic, black, tie shoe, but they were black and the toes were covered. The soles were flatter than what I am accustomed to, but I signed, "These are the ones I will wear."

Christine smiled again and shook her head. In sign, she said, "Yes, they will be all right!"

After shopping for about three hours, we went to a nice restaurant for lunch. I felt out of place everywhere we went! I believe because of my life with the Amish, people seem so different here.

At 4:00 p.m. we met Sue and she took us back to Christine's apartment. Christine was happy and we laughed our gurgling sounds and signed how comical it was to watch people watch us!

"Christine, you have adapted well to this life. I see you fitting right in with everyone. I, on the other hand, will never fit in."

"Collie, give yourself some time! It is difficult for you because you have been sheltered for so long." She then said, "I would like to go to church tomorrow. Would you?"

I signed. "Do you have a family of Christians who meet often and worship at each other's homes?"

"No," Christine signed. "I go to church about one and a half blocks from here. We will attend the 10:30 service, if that is okay with you. It is a small Lutheran church called St. Paul."

I laid down to rest, reflecting on the day and wishing I was back in Indiana. I realized I had to give myself more time and more space away from Isaiah before I could ever think about returning to Indiana again – if I ever do.

The next morning I awoke earlier than Christine. I was accustomed to getting up early for chores, so I made coffee and read her morning paper. I read something about the legendary Sunset Strip in Hollywood.

Christine entered the room and I asked, "What is this Strip?"

She signed, "The Strip begins and ends at the West Hollywood city limits. It is a very popular commuter route between Beverly Hills and Hollywood. It is considered the place to go for the entertainment world. It is the home of fancy restaurants, nightclubs, hotels, and expensive family residences. It is also famous as the stars' nightlife destination. You saw a small portion yesterday when we were shopping. I will fill you in later on some of the stories about West Hollywood. We now need to eat breakfast and get ready for church."

We walked to church since it was a clear day with beautiful blue skies. Flowers were everywhere and the smells were fragrant. I was basking in the sunshine and thanking God for my friendship with

Christine. Our friendship will sustain me through this turbulent period in my life. We entered St. Paul Lutheran Church and Peter was there waiting. We were seated midway down the aisle where we could see the pastor better.

The choir and organist sat in a balcony behind us. I was disappointed I would be unable to hear the music, but was uplifted when I saw a sign instructor go to the front to assist with the service. My heart skipped a beat when Pastor Jack Webb came out and took a seat. The words to the music were beautiful and placed within my mind the Word of God above all other thoughts.

Pastor Webb began to preach and the translator signed beautifully. It was a good sermon. He preached on Romans 10:9-10, that if you confess with your mouth that Jesus is Lord and believe in your heart God raised Him from the dead, you will be saved. Pastor Webb continued with verse 10: "For it is with your heart that you believe and are justified, and it is with your mouth that you confess and are saved."

My mind began to wander and I remember what Bishop Samuel Nolt preached at Anna Troyer's family home in Indiana. Isaiah had signed to me, "The Bishop asked, 'Who are justified?' All who believe are justified," Acts 13:39. "A man is not justified by the works of the law but by faith in Jesus Christ. Galatians 2:16 is where we look for justification."

Both the Bishop and Pastor Webb preached the same Bible verses. It made me happy and homesick to hear these wonderful men of God preach the same Scripture, no matter if it is done in a Lutheran church or an Amish home. Faith involves inward belief as well as outward confessions. This has become clearer to me as time passes and I talk with my Lord every day.

At the end of the service on our way out, Pastor Webb smiled at me and gave me a very firm handshake and a hug. Peter and Christine were surprised when they found out I had sat with him on the whole trip out west.

"What a small world," Peter wrote to me. "God took you under His wing once again and watched over you, Collie! It was definitely no coincidence that you two were seated together!"

127

We made a promise to Pastor Webb that we would invite him for dinner. He thanked us and was pleased to know Christine was the friend with whom I had come to stay. He told Peter to tell me he would make sure there would be an interpreter at each service.

The following week, Christine and I walked all over the area. She knew a lot of people, and I could tell by the warm receptions she was well liked. We sat on the beach and watched people.

"Christine, tell me some of the stories about West Hollywood."

Christine signed, "This is a pet-friendly place. Almost everyone has some kind of pet."

I noticed many dogs as we walked.

Christine said, "There is a lease agreement that states a person 62 years old or older may keep up to two pets. Some stipulations apply to others as well. Many West Hollywood hotels are pet-welcoming. They even offer pet amenities, such as bowls, treats, and beds and will arrange for a dog walker if needed.

"West Hollywood also boasts the largest single population. There are 35,000 full- time residents, and, on the weekend, the population rises from 50,000 to 75,000. Nearby communities take advantage of shopping, dining, and entertainment. When you need to go downtown or to the beach, it is only 12 miles away. I try to walk every day and enjoy

sitting on the beach with an iced drink to watch people. I really love it here, Collie!"

"I am so happy for you, Christine! I feel the same way about Indiana and the Amish people. I have never spent a winter anywhere else, but maybe I would like this weather year-round. I will find out this year. However, right now my heart is still heavy and back in Indiana with Isaiah and his family."

Chapter 36

The Studio

I stared out into space and began to think. I wonder if Isaiah and Rachel are still seeing each other. I wonder if Rachel and her family have moved. I wonder a lot of things, but I know I must put my trust in God to direct my path in accordance with His plan.

The next day, Christine and I took another walk. She signed, "Collie, tomorrow will be Wednesday, and, true to my word, I will return to the studio to work. I want you to go along, meet everyone, and see what I do." I agreed.

When I watched Christine at the studio, she was good! She signed for the people whose characters were not the main characters. They called them "fill-ins" or "extras" who were needed for the picture. She understood her assignments and followed through with the deaf-mute characters to the point I understood the storyline and their role in the film. It was very interesting! Peter's acting was like a magnet drawing everyone into his role.

The following day, and then again on Friday, I observed all Christine did. She had opulent energy and seemed to be everywhere at once. Peter clearly loved her and she him in return. They will marry someday, I thought, as I watched them. When that happens, I will have to make a life for myself here in California or go back to Indiana – maybe even somewhere in between. Once again, I pondered my life – where I came from and where I will be going.

A month or so has now passed. When Christine and I were walking to the studio one day, I thought I saw someone I knew walking toward us. Pointing, I signed, "Christine, do you know that man?"

Looking up, she signed, "No, he's probably a movie star. They're all over the studio grounds, surrounding the sets."

He disappeared into another studio next to where Christine was working. I pondered all evening over who he could have been.

Later, I signed to Christine, "I do not know any movie stars. In Indiana, I led a sheltered life, remember? I never watched television, or went to movies, yet something about that man looked familiar. Maybe we will see him again. I will get a closer look and perhaps recognize him."

Putting those thoughts aside for now, Christine showed me the script for tomorrow so I could help her instruct the deaf actors and actresses on getting their lines signed correctly. Sometimes it proved to be a difficult task, because some of them were not deaf mutes. They only acted that way to win the part.

I enjoyed the work, and the pay was very good. I was able to save a lot of money and still pay Christine something for living with her in her apartment. I felt relatively happy working with deaf actors and actresses, but it made me miss the children at school. I knew school would be starting soon and it made it more difficult to be away. I wondered if Isaiah's hearing had gotten worse. My thoughts were good thoughts when I fell asleep.

In the morning, Christine and I hurried to work. When I finished the day and returned home to the apartment, I found a letter from Deborah.

"Dear Collie, nothing seems to make sense since you left for California. We all miss you so much!" She drew a picture of the "I Love You" sign. I smiled at the picture as I continued to read.

"The work around here never seems to end! You may remember Daed and my brothers are in the field from dawn to dusk. They are presently in the wheat field, and it will soon be time for the harvest.

Daed and Maem are too busy to write, but you will soon hear from Maem. Ruth and Leah are baking today. I swept the porch and hung out the laundry. Maem needs all of our help because she is so busy. Amos still does not court anyone. Jacob likes Sadie Yoder. Joseph is pretending he is too busy for girls, but you know he likes them too much to act like he doesn't! Isaiah and Rachel still see each other. Isaiah said, 'We are friends.' Rachel and her family bought a farm about a mile or two from ours. We have church at their house, when it is their turn. I am still not interested in anyone, but I do think Louis Graber is nice. We all miss you, Collie. Write to me soon. Love, Deborah."

I remember Sadie Yoder. She is the sister of the young teacher who replaced Lizzie Farmwald when she became ill during the school year. I believe her sister's name is Anna. She and Jacob would be a good match, I thought. Of course I knew Rachel and Isaiah are friends. Most people are before they become married, aren't they?

Christine signed, "Collie, there is a surgical specialist in Los Angles who might look at us both to see about our deafness. He might even be able to help us hear. Will you go with me if I can set up an appointment?" I agreed.

One month later, we arrived at Dr. Thomas Yarnell's office. Peter drove us. Many lengthy tests were done on us both and, once again, the audiologist wrote on a piece of paper that most likely I inherited my deafness and it cannot be reversed. I must accept that I will never hear or speak! I really never allowed myself to become too eager for good news, because somehow I knew I would never be healed this side of heaven! However, Christine was quite hopeful. She was born a deaf mute, but the audiologist didn't think hers was as severe as mine. He explained to her in writing that they have cochlear implants that help some deaf people. He would like to do further testing to see if she would be a good candidate. She was afraid to be hopeful yet. However, I could see she was already hoping it would be her answer to either living forever deaf, or being able to hear. He made arrangements for us to stay close to the hospital clinic so Christine could have more tests the following day.

We had an early dinner and went to our motel room. We signed each other until very late that night. I prayed Christine would be a good candidate for the implants.

The next day, after the testing was completed, we went to lunch and discussed in sign the advantages and disadvantages of getting implants. The cost to have it done is expensive! I saw Christine's face when the doctor wrote that high-powered hearing aids could cost a couple thousand dollars, but cochlear implants can be several thousand dollars.

After lunch, we returned to Dr. Yarnell's office for her test results. He wrote that she had profound unilateral, not bilateral, hearing loss. That makes a cochlear implant virtually impossible. There is no one who knows if her hearing loss is due to genetics. Never having worn a hearing aid before was against her, too. He could not guarantee it would work.

Christine and I thanked him and we left feeling disappointed. I really felt bad for her! If she could have had the implants, her life with Peter and her occupation would have benefited. Christine, being the wonderful person she is, accepted the inevitable and thanked God for the opportunity to get the tests and settle her mind and heart as to whether she could have been medically helped.

Peter picked us up for a wonderful dinner before returning to Hollywood. I was in admiration of the gentleness he displayed toward Christine. He did not offer her sympathy, but, instead, displayed a spirit of love, as he signed with her and held her in between signing, giving her the emotional support she needed.

At work the next day, Christine was right back into being everywhere at once helping the entire cast as only she can. It was all I could do just to keep up with the instructions she gave me! She continually signed, "Collie, God has a plan for your life." She is always showing me her love and trust in our Lord Jesus Christ.

Chapter 37

Bobby Collins

A few days later, in the parking lot, as we were leaving the studio, I, once again, saw the man I thought I knew. Christine did not know him. As we drew near, I recognized who he was – Bobby Collins, my brother through adoption. I was so surprised to see him! At first he wasn't sure who I was, and then I saw recognition come into his eyes. He actually hugged me! Christine and I signed and clapped our hands out of happiness. We were in shock that we were all together in California.

Peter came to pick us up and we all went back into the studio lunchroom. Peter talked to Bobby and fielded our questions. Bobby said Karen had died from cancer and Steve remarried a few years later. Rita, our foster sister, is married, but he has lost touch with her and does not know where she lives. We still could not believe we were seeing one another in Hollywood, California, of all places! He said the last he had heard, I was in Fort Wayne, Indiana.

Peter asked what he was doing here. Bobby said he is still playing guitar, in a band, and is traveling a lot. But, he is now doing a movie, a small part, and enjoys it. Peter told him he might be able to help him go a little further in the field of acting if he's interested.

Bobby could not believe I had lived with the Amish people in Indiana. He told Peter he had heard of the Amish, but never met them or had been around them. He wanted to know why I came out here. Peter explained that Christine and I were long-time friends and we all need a change from time to time. He smiled and said he was happy for me.

We were both excited to see one another once again and hoped to get together very soon. But I knew we would probably never meet again. The realization of our

differences came to mind: the hearing and the non-hearing! I hugged him goodbye and Peter gave him his telephone number.

I received a letter from Jeanna today. "Dear Collie, I am expecting another baby and we are very happy. Our son, Zachary, is adorable! Enclosed is a photograph of Kevin, Zachary, and me. I am bragging an awful lot aren't I?"

They looked so happy!

"I am still working as a dispatcher for the police, and Kevin has been promoted and is doing well. We had to build on a small addition to make room for our new baby. Do you hear from Isaiah? I often think of the two of you and believe God will see that you meet someone who will make you happy, if He hasn't already. Write when you can. We love you, Jeanna and family."

I sat right down and answered her with a quick note, leaving out that Isaiah and Rachel, I am pretty sure, are a couple by now. I told her I had not heard from Isaiah since moving to California. I had to get ready for work, so I said I would write later. "I love you and am very happy for your news about the baby. Love in Christ, Collie."

Today, Christine suggested we go to the beach. We got everything ready and she had her neighbor, Sue, call the taxi company. I worried about the expense, but Christine said, "Do not give it another thought! I have enough money that we can enjoy our day."

The beach was so big and the water was absolutely beautiful! "I have never seen anything like this," I signed to her.

She smiled and, in sign, told me when she and Peter were first dating they came here frequently; however, his work now keeps him so much busier than her that he can't come as often. I felt the sadness when she explained to me their time together is so precious. I can see why, due to their different work schedules.

We stayed at the beach for only three hours, as we did not want to get sunburned. Especially with Christine's red hair! I enjoyed the afternoon and thanked her so much. She told me to prepare for Saturday, when we go on the Hollywood walking tour. In sign I asked, "What is that?" She explained that over 2,000 movie stars, singers, comedians, actors, and even Mickey Mouse, have their star on the "Hollywood Walk of Fame."

"It sounds interesting to me," I signed. "Right now, though, I just want to take a shower and rest." I am used to being in the sun from working in the garden in Indiana, but the beach is overwhelming! With so many people and so much water, the heat seems more intense. Even though it is beautiful in California, I still longed for the simple, plain life in Indiana.

The following day, Christine and I took another taxi to the Hollywood Walking Tour. "It was created in 1958," she explained, "and is spread out quite a long way!" It was also crowded with street performers and sales people, who bothered us as we walked along. We saw several homeless people as well. I looked at them and thought, without the grace of God, I could have been one of them!

Christine signed, "As I previously mentioned, there are over 2,000 stars displayed up and down Hollywood and Vine Streets, covering a distance of about two miles. A lot of the stars most people have never heard of are covered by dirt and are not legible. Would you like to have your picture taken among them?"

I signed, "Absolutely not! My Old Order Amish way of believing does not allow picture taking."

Christine reminded me that I am not Amish; yet, in my heart, I always will be!

Christine signed, "There is no way we can cover the entire 'Walk of Fame.' We will see a lot of people dressed up, trying to make us believe they are stars."

We were growing weary and decided to return to the apartment. When we got settled in, I signed, "It seems to me that Hollywood is for the rich. And those who are not rich seem to be homeless. It is definitely a disparity and not my kind of place to live."

A few weeks later, we traveled to Mount Lee to get a closer look at the famous Hollywood sign. Mount Lee is one of the peaks in the Santa Monica Mountains. There are many hiking trails that go to the Hollywood sign. However, actual access close enough is fenced off. On a clear day, when you reach the top, you can see all of Los Angeles. It is quite breathtaking! The Pacific Ocean, in the background, is quite a sight to see!

I signed to Christine, "Here again, this is one of the most beautiful sights I have ever seen! Thank you for this day. It will remain in my heart and mind forever! Being in your company and seeing this creation our Lord has provided for us is absolutely wonderful!"

Later, I explained to Christine, "Being a Christian, I know you will understand my way of thinking. When we went to the 'Walk of Fame,' I saw worldly people being idolized. But, when we went to the top of Mount Lee to see the Hollywood sign, in the background I saw the Pacific Ocean, God's creation. The beauty is that God made it for all of mankind to see. I failed to see that same beauty on the 'Walk of Fame.'"

Christine hugged me and smiled as she signed, "Collie, you are definitely Amish!"

The following week, one of the cast members fell off the stage during rehearsal. She was one of the deaf women who had a significant role. Christine had worked diligently with her for several weeks. We all felt bad for her as the ambulance pulled away to take her to the hospital. Our dinner that evening was full of discussion about her.

Peter signed, "Sue will not be able to finish the movie. Christine, who can you recommend as her replacement? Do you know someone who can enliven the part she was playing?"

Christine signed, "I will work through the cast tomorrow and pull someone who has impressive signing abilities. Let me think on it tonight."

After dinner, I went to my room to allow Peter and Christine some much-deserved alone time. I decided to write to Rebekah, as it had been quite a while since we last communicated.

"Dear Rebekah, I have been ever so busy and apologize for not writing sooner. I am wondering how you, Joshua, and the family are getting along. I can imagine how busy you all are! I have missed working in the garden, canning, and the harvest time. Summer is almost over and school will soon be starting. I imagine Leah will be the only one in school this fall. Who has been teaching the deaf children?

"This past year and a half has gone by quickly; yet, I feel as though I have been here forever! I hope Joshua is enjoying good health. Give my love to everyone and write when you have time. Fill me in on the neighbors, the Bishops, friends, and, especially, the family. I love and miss you all so much! I am being faithful in my Scripture reading and church attendance. The pastor at the church we attend is Pastor Jack Webb. He is a fine man of God. God is good! Love in Christ, Collie."

The next day, Christine signed to me, "I have two women in mind to replace Sue. When they come in, I will show you who they are. Will you watch them today, while I watch the deaf cast, and see which one is better?"

I did as Christine asked and signed, "Neither one really stood out the way Sue did. Is there someone else in the group who you think can manage what is expected of them?"

She signed, "Not yet. I have worked with this same group for months, but am troubled by the cast! Sue was chosen for her ability to follow directions accurately and with enthusiasm. She is so much better than the others!"

Peter signed, "The shooting for this film can be done around them this week. Let's hope by the end of the week, someone will come forward who really wants this part and will work harder than the others to reflect the character in a positive way."

During the next couple of days, we worked hard with all of them. We were still unable to find the spark we needed from even one let alone give the performance that was of vital importance to the making of the film! Christine and I were both exhausted, and even Peter was ready to call it a day.

He signed, "Both of you go home and rest. I will stop by later. Don't fix dinner, because I will pick up something." I was beginning to get spoiled, as Peter always found the best restaurants with the best take-out food.

Christine and I rested after our showers and she chilled a bottle of wine for her and Peter. I had a bottle of diet cola chilling for me.

Peter arrived with Chinese food and it was wonderful! I preferred the fried chicken with rice and an eggroll. It was an enjoyable evening together. I excused myself and retired to bed, leaving them still discussing the right person for the movie.

I asked God to help us choose whomever He had in mind for us. I also prayed for my Indiana family and, as always, for Isaiah. I wondered if his hearing had changed a lot in the past year and a half. No one mentioned anything in the letters I had received.

I had nearly fallen asleep when, suddenly, I sat straight up in bed! I hurried into the living room and found Christine and Peter still discussing the cast.

I signed excitedly, "I know who would be perfect for Sue's role!"

They looked back at me and Christine signed," Who, you?"

"No, silly, you!"

Peter got up quickly and swung me around and signed, "Collie, you are a genius! Christine, you have been so busy teaching that it never occurred to me. Who knows this movie better than you? From beginning to end, this has been your calling."

Christine kept shaking her head no!

I signed, "Yes, yes, yes! You are so charming, attractive, winning, and unaffected by the stars around you. Don't you see, Christine? This role is meant and made for you!"

Christine signed, "It has been a long time for me to take up acting again."

Peter wrapped his arms around her. He stepped back and slowly formed his lips for her to read and understand. "Christine, I have been enchanted with you since the first time I saw you. I have watched you work with the deaf for this movie. You have displayed a joyous labor of love for all of us, to make everyone look good. As Collie said, you are perfect for this role!"

She looked up at him, smiled, and signed, "Okay, Peter, for you I will do it. I will do my best to achieve what you require. Thank you for your confidence in me. Collie, I will deal with you later!"

She hugged me and smiled as I left them alone and returned to bed. I slept better that night than I had in a long time.

The next day, Christine signed, "I am very nervous! Will the cast accept me?"

"Of course they will," I signed. "You have been a mentor to all of them for a long time."

We then had our breakfast, went to the studio, and entered the casting area. Upon our arrival, everyone clapped, and those who could speak yelled, smiled, and cheered. Christine cried!

Production was behind schedule since the accident, as filming had been shot entirely around Sue. The cast took their places and Christine signed, informing me, "Collie, you will take over my former position and teach the necessary lines. Welcome to show biz, my friend!"

The day passed quickly with some minor glitches, but, overall, we went home pleased with the day's activities.

Peter came over later and he, too, was quite happy with the positive reception Christine received and how quickly I was able to overcome my shyness and perform her duties.

Peter signed, "We should finish the movie within a few weeks. I wish to thank you both. By the way, Collie, Bobby came by today. His band is playing this weekend at one of the clubs. I thought you, Christine, and I could attend and enjoy his music. I realize neither of you can hear him play, but you have told me you feel the music in vibration. How about it, girls?"

We both looked at one another and signed, "Yea! We want to go!"

We arrived at the dance hall and were told that several different bands would be playing. When it was time for Bobby's band, "New Beginnings," the dance floor was crowded and everyone was clapping. We were caught up in the clapping and observing the dancers. Everyone was saying Bobby's band was good and Peter even said, "Very good!" We were all very proud of him!

Peter signed, "Bobby will travel a lot with 'New Beginnings' and see most of the United States, as well as possibly some countries abroad. Later, if he chooses not to become an actor, he can always fall back on his music career."

We decided to leave early, as we were faced with another busy day on set. What a lovely and productive day we had. In my prayers, I will thank God and ask Him to bless Bobby in his career desires.

I laid in bed reflecting on my time in California. I must confess, I have had some wonderful moments here. Christine has shown me a lot of interesting places and has been a wonderful hostess and friend. The movie has been a wonderful experience to work on with Christine. I remember her saying there will be a grand opening and I will not believe the movie stars, actors, musicians, producers, and directors who will attend. I now see that this is her world, and I am happy for her and Peter. As for me, my heart and world is still in Indiana! I also wonder if Isaiah and Rachel are married and about my future. I do not worry, just wonder, because I trust in the Lord and will continue to follow Him as He directs my path home to be with Him someday. There will be my true and precious love!

Sunday at church, Pastor Webb asked Peter to sign to me and inquire if I would be interested in beginning a sign class for children. He remembered I had told him about my teaching in Indiana. We set a time to begin the class on Wednesday evening at 6:00. This day and time would not interfere with my present schedule. If anything needed to be changed, Pastor Webb would definitely accommodate my work schedule.

I was excited to return to teaching! I sat in my room that evening and remembered how much I loved to teach. I decided to begin with the alphabet signs. I found using those letters gave the scholars the best advantages in learning manual spelling. I picked up some notebooks and began preparing for my first lesson.

There were only three children to begin: ages five, seven, and eight. They were eager to learn and cooperated completely. During the teaching session, their parents would sometimes join us. The children would laugh at them trying to learn and sign, and their lives at home became more fun for all. What a blessing God gave me! My handicap has finally become a useful tool to help others!

Chapter 38

Peter and Christine
Announce Their Marriage

The weeks flew by and the movie was finished. It was exhausting and exhilarating, but Christine shined in her role. I was so very proud of her and to be an active part of it!

Christine signed, "Next week will be the movie release. They call it a premiere or first performance. That simply means it can be a play, ballet, or any number of other worthwhile events."

I signed, "Will everyone who made the movie be there?"

"Oh yes," Christine signed, "movie stars, producers, directors, and playwrights. The audience will be full of all kinds of professional people, from New York City to Los Angeles."

"Are you nervous?" I asked.

"Yes, Collie, very nervous! I want this movie to be a hit for everyone who gave of their God-given talent, time, sweat, and tears."

I signed, "Let us pray right at this moment for God's blessing to be upon it."

We did just that. Then we hugged and were comforted as only God can provide. We celebrated by going shopping and purchasing some beautiful gowns.

"Collie, it was a smash! Tomorrow's newspapers will be full of wonderful reviews and I can finally say, 'I made it! My dreams have come true.' You have been a wonderful friend! Because of your assistance, love, sharing, and everything else you have done with me, I am forever in your debt! Your insight to urge me to do the role after Sue fell gave me the courage to know how good I could be!"

I hugged her and signed, "When God speaks to us Christians, we must listen!"

Christine had great reviews in the papers the next day and Peter was beside himself with happiness for her, as was I.

A week went by when I signed, "Christine, the movie star life is not for me. The glamour is not in alignment with my beliefs and what I want for myself. I am very unsettled about my future, yet I believe, as I have for many years (even back to when I was molested in the park), that God has a plan for me. I believe it because, at that point in my life, you told me He did, and I know to this day it has not been fulfilled. I am asking you to pray for me. I am in need of an answer to the dilemma I face right now."

"Collie, my dearest friend, I will definitely pray more specifically for you and for Him to answer your prayers. God will answer our prayers!"

The following day, as we attended Pastor Webb's church, I handed him a letter with the same request I had given to Christine. He smiled and wrote in return that he would definitely pray in faith for me. He told Peter to tell me that God's plan for my life would come to fruition by faith. I was excited, because I remember Joshua telling Isaiah and Isaiah signing to me that "the actual fervent prayer of a righteous man avails much," James 5:16. I cannot think of a more righteous man in Hollywood, California, than Pastor Jack Webb.

Now that the movie was finished, I found I had a lot of time on my hands. I began visiting a shelter for battered women called Rolling Acres. I worked in the office – filing, typing, and organizing some of the voluminous paperwork the government required. The women could not sign, but soon learned we could exchange written notes. They wrote to me asking questions about my handicap and I, in turn, wrote back, asking about their challenges.

One young woman named Katrina wrote me a lengthy letter describing an abusive boyfriend. She feared him greatly and wondered if when she left the shelter he would be waiting for her. He had threatened to kill her many times in the past. I listened, unable to comprehend the kind of hatred he had for her. I shared with her my molestation experience of many years ago. Through commonality, we became friends and spent time together.

Katrina is only 30 years old and already feels her life is over. I encouraged her to read her Bible. We passed many notes attempting to work our way through non-conformity to the world. We must trust in God and His ways.

After about a month, Katrina began to understand God's grace! I wrote her that God says, in Luke 6:2, "Love your enemies." The heart of Jesus' teaching is love! I said, "You do not have to go back to the abusive situation you were in. You can still love your boyfriend, who is now your enemy, and pray that God will change him, but you must try to move on to something or someone else. I pray for the man who molested me. He is in jail, or was in jail, for multiple offensive charges against me and others. I pray God will help him! It took me years before I could ask for forgiveness for hating him. Now I try and see him as God sees him, His child, created in His image, and forgiven!"

I noticed the duties of the women at Rolling Acres are meaningful to them. Some cook, some clean, some do laundry, but whatever task they perform, they feel as useful as they would at home.

Rolling Acres is surrounded by palm trees, rolling hills, flowers of all types, and numerous birds and butterflies are abundant. The whole atmosphere displays a serenity of peace. All of the women who reside here need to feel the peace of God that passes all understanding. I feel that peace and pray for each and every one of them to experience the same contentment I experience.

When we awoke in the morning, Christine told me she and Peter are getting married on March 12. I am so happy for them! In sign I asked, "Are you having a large wedding?"

She shook her head and signed, "No, we are not going to make it a big event after such a large movie premier! I would like you to be my maid of honor, Collie."

I signed, "I would be delighted. Yes! Do you know where you will have the wedding?"

"We have already talked to Pastor Webb, and he has agreed to marry us. Norma, the lady who signs at church, has agreed to help with the ceremony. I will be nervous to read lips through the exchanging of vows! We won't need music, since you and I cannot hear, and Peter is okay with that."

"Will you live at Peter's?" I asked.

She responded, "We haven't decided yet, but, most likely, we will live here at my place since it is closer to the studio and I am familiar with the surroundings. You will remain here with us because we want you here. The only change is that Peter will live here, also. Maybe next week we can go shopping for shoes for the wedding. Peter is going to ask Bobby to be his best man. He has many good friends, but he thought it was more pleasing for the four of us to be together."

"I look forward to being a part of such a memorable important day. Thank you both for wanting Bobby and me to participate!"

The following day when I went to the shelter, I wrote a note to Mrs. Bherns and told her of the upcoming wedding of my best friend. I mentioned that her husband will be living with us from now on. She replied back in a note, offering a remarkable solution for me, Christine, and Peter.

She wrote, "Collie, beside the shelter is an empty apartment. If you would be interested in renting it, I would like you to have your own place. It would place you closer to observe what goes on at Rolling Acres and would also place you nearby so when you work later than scheduled, you can slip out the door and be home quickly. I think it is a win/win for everyone concerned. You think about it and let me know what you decide."

The idea delighted me, as Peter and Christine would have their privacy and I would have some independence. I wrote back to Mrs. Bherns that I do not need to think about it. "I accept and thank you so much!" My goodness, when God has a plan, He quickly puts events into action!

I returned home to find Christine and Peter discussing their honeymoon plans. I walked in with the biggest smile and they both looked at me. Christine signed, "Collie, you look like if you could only speak you would be a chatterbox right now!"

I signed, "You are very intuitive! Next week, I will be moving into an apartment next to Rolling Acres!"

Christine signed, "What! You know you are welcome to stay with us. What are you thinking Collie?"

I signed, "I am thinking I want my own place, where I can sit back and think of my newly-married best friends enjoying each other and a life of being together as married couples deserve to be, as in *two*. Be happy for me! I am delighted! The apartment will suit me just fine and I will be close to the ladies I have become so fond of. How many times have we discussed God's timing in situations? This is an example of another one!"

They both shook their heads and we laughed our infamous gurgling sounds, making Peter laugh. Then we made hot chocolate, as I marveled at what a day this has been!

Christine and I began shopping for wedding dresses and shoes. Christine found a beautiful ivory, calf-length dress with cap sleeves and a sash around the waist. It was perfect for her! She also found an ivory-colored hat to match, with a short veil that comes down over her eyes. I found a rose-colored, calf-length dress with an ivory sash around it. Quite beautiful! I didn't purchase a hat because Christine said I would not need one. We both bought matching ivory shoes. Christine's heels were taller than mine, as I preferred lower to flat-heeled shoes, which I was accustomed to wearing.

After our purchases, we stopped in a coffee shop for lunch. Some of the cast members we had taught were there. Our sign language friends were happy to see us! They were excited that Christine and Peter were getting married. Christine was with a selective group of people she was comfortable with and would remain with for years to come, while she and Peter remained in show business. We then left for home carrying our purchases. When we arrived, we sat down, put our feet up, and were satisfied with our day.

Christine signed, "Collie, I am thinking about another movie soon. Would you help and be willing to be a big part of it?"

In sign, I admitted to Christine, "Movies are not for me! I enjoyed this one only because we did it together! I have a greater interest in Rolling Acres Homeless Shelter. I hope that doesn't upset you, Christine, but I feel God is going to change my life's course once again. All of my new direction seems to point towards the shelter. I will still see you often and come by the studio, if that's all right?"

"You are a special person, Collie, and I know whatever you choose to do will be pleasing to the Lord. I will look forward to seeing you on the set with me every day possible. You have always been an inspiration to me and always will be!"

When I retired to my room, I asked God, "Is the shelter where you want me to be?" In my heart, God spoke to me. He said, "Your motive in giving is to help your fellow man and bring glory to me. You can do that no matter what direction you choose for your life. Always strive to bring glory to me!"

Chapter 39

The Letter

Next Saturday is the wedding! I'm so excited and have a lot to do. Everything Christine and I need to buy for the wedding has already been purchased. Today, I am going to pack all of my personal belongings and move into the apartment adjacent to the shelter. It will take a couple of days to get settled in, but I'm looking forward to this next chapter in my life. I'm sure I will experience some loneliness but also know I am doing the right thing. I bought some small things for my room while living with Christine and, today, Peter is moving them for me. I know he is anxious to be moving as well. As I was getting luggage out of the closet, Christine tapped on my door and opened it. I noticed she had a letter for me in her hand. I thanked her and opened the letter.

"Dear Collette, I am sorry it has taken me so long to write. I want to share what is happening here. You may know, as Deborah may have written, that Jacob and Sadie Yoder began courting about a year ago. They are now married and bought land about three miles from us. Joseph and a sweet, young maidel (girl) met at one of the singings. Her name is Sarah Miller now. She is an older sister of one of your former students, Anna Troyer. We are happy they have married and bought land about five miles from us."

I pondered what was written and had trouble following all that had happened during my absence these past three and a half years!

Rebekah continued, "Deborah and Louis Graber are getting along quite well. I will not be surprised if they marry next. Now, I have saved the most interesting for last! Amos and Rachel fell in love and married about six months ago."

Upon reading this, I dropped the letter! What could my maem be telling me? What happened to Rachel and Isaiah? I thought they would be married by now and have a child. I grabbed the letter and ran into the living room to Christine. I was unable to stop signing too fast and crying at the same time!

Christine grabbed my hands, "Collie, calm down, what is the matter with you?"

I pointed to the letter and signed, "Amos and Rachel got married!"

"What happened to Rachel and Isaiah?" Christine signed. "Go finish the letter, Collie."

I ran back to my room and continued reading. "Collette, Isaiah's hearing steadily gets worse, yet he never complains. We do see a change in him, though. He always professed that he and Rachel were just good friends. Do you remember him saying the exact same thing to you? On the other hand, Amos has always loved Rachel, even as a child. But we all thought she had an eye for Isaiah and, in her heart, wanted him to be her husband. Does this event change anything for you as far as coming back to Indiana? Maybe you have met someone in California you are happy with. I should have written you long ago about the marriages, but I was so busy with all of the wedding preparations and work at home. I was also overwhelmed with my three elder sons marrying! I hope you understand! I know you would have tried to come back to Indiana, but I know you have been busy in California and I didn't want you to feel obligated to come back. Financially, I'm sure, it wasn't feasible as well.

"Amos and Rachel moved to LaGrange, Indiana. They are close enough that we visit them when we have time. Their church District is not in our District, but we see them whenever possible. They are very happy, and Isaiah is happy for them."

Amos and Rachel are married? I cannot believe what I am reading! *Amos* and Rachel are married?

"Collette, we miss you and wish you were here with us. I had hoped by now you would be tired of California and have missed us enough to return home. I want you to know, dochtah (daughter), that if at any time you want to come home to live again, we want you to return. If we had the money to fly you home, I would send you a ticket like Christine did, when you left here to join her there. Maybe if you decide to come back, we can arrange financially for your return. Let me know what you want to do. Regardless of your decision, though, we love and miss you. Love, Rebekah."

I cried throughout reading the letter. I went into the living room where Christine was waiting for my return. I gave the letter to her to read and when she was done, she hugged me, cried with me, and we sat for the longest time. At last she signed, "Collie, what do you want to do?"

In sign I replied, "I have loved Isaiah from the first moment I saw him. I need to go home!"

The sobs continued. When I was composed enough to rationalize my feelings, I signed, "I will remain here for the wedding this week and when you both leave for your honeymoon, I will fly back to Indiana. I made enough money from the movie to last for many years. Perhaps you and Peter can help me make the flight arrangements. I do have one request, though. When you make the arrangements, would you see if you can route me through Indianapolis where I once lived?"

Christine signed, "Of course we will make all of the arrangements. Whatever you want my dear friend!"

I lied in bed and thought about the letter and all of the events that took place over the past 13 months here in California and back home in Indiana. I am so homesick to see my family! I thanked God once again for the direction in which He is taking my life.

The next day, Christine and Peter were able to book the flight and purchase my ticket. I have a four-hour layover in Indianapolis and then fly into Fort Wayne, Indiana. My concern is, when I arrive in Fort Wayne, how do I get to Shipshewana?

Christine came home later and informed me that Peter had spoken to Kevin and Jeanna at the Fort Wayne Police Department, where they both work. They will pick me up at the airport and drive me to Shipshewana to Joshua and Rebekah's home on Monday morning. The reality of what is about to happen brought me to my knees! Once again, I was amazed. When God has a plan, He quickly places it into action!

I visited the shelter and explained in a note to Mrs. Bherns about the change of events in my life. She understood my desire to return home and wrote back, "You are a special person, Collie, and I have been praying for you. I could see something was missing in your life. When you speak of Isaiah, I now understand that he is the 'something' missing. God bless you on your journey!"

I returned to the apartment and laid my luggage on the bed. Some of the items I owned could be packed. I was eager to get out of the clothes I had worn when I came here, so I washed them and hung them up to dry. I smiled as I pulled out my black, tie shoes. I like them so much! When I opened the second piece of luggage, I was startled! There were two letters in the pocket of the luggage. I couldn't believe I had forgotten they were there! They were the last two letters I saved to read if I were to get homesick. One was from Amos and the other was from Rachel. I opened the one from Amos first.

"Dear Collie, you are leaving for California tomorrow. I cannot imagine living our lives without you being a part of them. I have been thinking a lot about leaving also. I am now 21 years old and really should have my own land and farm. However, I hope to find someone to share it with first. No one else knows what I am sharing with you in this letter. I have been in love with Rachel for a long time, even when we were young kids and they came to stay with us. However, it seems she has always had eyes for Isaiah. I also know you are in love with him, as I watched you and him together. You taught us your language and were eager to learn our plain folk ways. You even learned our Pennsylvania Dutch! I marveled at how quickly you adapted to our customs. I believe Isaiah loves you, and has loved you since the time he brought you here to live with us."

I stopped reading and began crying. My thoughts were did you love me Isaiah? How could I have missed the signs? Was I so accustomed to rejection throughout my growing years that I missed the sign of love when it actually came to me? Have I allowed my pride to keep us apart all of these years? I pray not!

Amos continued, "Rachel looked my way sometimes and I became more confused. She seemed to take an interest in me, yet I see her laughing and walking with Isaiah and she appears happy and content. I will admit, I am confused and need to sort this all out. Maybe I will leave for a while and meet someone I want to marry someday. I hope you are happy in California. We miss you already and think about you a lot! Write to me when you can. By the way, I changed your cat's name from Lokka to Faul. I was tired of hearing everyone yell Lokka. In case you did not know, Lokka means to call, as in, 'Here kitty kitty.' So when we call out Lokka, every cat in the area comes around! Faul suits her better. In Deutsch it means 'lazy.' She sleeps, stretches, eats, and naps again after she eats. Then she lies around some more. She is not a good mouser either! Love, Amos."

I laughed as I pictured all of the cats and kittens running toward the person yelling Lokka. I imagined everyone laughing at the scene. It makes me even more homesick! I then opened Rachel's letter.

"Dear Collie, I have not been here long enough to become acquainted with you the way I had hoped. I am sorry you will be leaving tomorrow. I hope you find happiness with your friend in California. Isaiah said she is a very nice person and you have been friends for many years. Unfortunately, I have never had many friends or anyone with whom I remotely felt close. When my parents came here to find a home and be close to friends, I was excited. I liked you right away! I asked Isaiah to teach me sign language so we could communicate. He was eager to show me and we spent a great deal of time together before you left, because I wanted to learn your language quickly. I always had a desire to be with Isaiah and maybe someday get married, but life is funny sometimes. When we got here, I could see he had a lot of feelings for you. At first I was jealous, until I saw the two of you together and knew there was more than friendship involved. I also noticed the way Amos looked at me was also the way I looked at Amos. I hope you realize I am trying to tell you that I want to be with Amos more than Isaiah. Isaiah also wants to be with you more than with me! I will continue to learn your language and, when you return, if you return, we can sign together and become friends. I hope so! Love, Rachel."

I sat back and realized that one and a half years have passed. Amos and Rachel are married and I did not know Isaiah cared for me more than I was aware. What could I have done? I wanted to get away quickly and, in doing so, did I lose Isaiah? I pray not!

I will return to Indiana on Monday morning. I am so excited! I went into the living room and signed to Christine. "Please pray for me and Isaiah, that we will get together after all." I signed to her some parts of the letter so she could better understand.

"God works in mysterious ways doesn't He, Collie?"

Saturday arrived and Peter picked us up to go to St. Paul Lutheran Church, where Pastor Jack Webb was waiting. A few flowers were placed near the altar. The service was conducted by Pastor Webb with Peter, Christine, Bobby, and Norma the interpreter in attendance. After the service was over, Christine and I signed our goodbyes and cried. They then departed on their honeymoon. I stayed on to share my plans with Pastor Webb about returning to Indiana on Monday.

Pastor held me and Norma signed, "He has enjoyed meeting you, Collie. It was the most memorable plane trip he has ever taken. He asks that you continue to communicate with him and let him know what happens in your life. He also said he would pray for you and your young man, Isaiah. He says he will pray for you both to marry, if that is the plan God has worked out for you."

I embraced him, signing goodbye, then Bobby and I walked out of the church together. I knew I would probably never see Bobby again, so I wrote him a letter the night before. I told him how happy I was for him. I said I pray he will achieve his life's ambition with music and film. He put the letter in his pocket, hugged me goodbye, and walked away with tears in his eyes.

The next morning, Christine's neighbor arranged for the taxi to take me to the airport. I gave her the key, as was prearranged. I had a 5 x 7 chalkboard in my carry-on bag in case I needed to seek directions. I was on the plane less afraid this time after having flown once before, to come to California.

I reread Rebekah's letter. I had no apprehension that I would be welcome again, even though I would surprise them! But I wondered about Isaiah's reaction. I hoped he would be excited and in good spirits. My thoughts turned to the front of the plane as the stewardess pointed for me to look at the monitor to fasten my seatbelt. We were landing in Indianapolis. I had a four-hour layover, wondering what I would do with all that time.

I began to remember some of my past. I reflected on the memories I had before I was adopted by Steve and Karen Collins. Karen mentioned to me once a name I was trying to recollect, but I was unable to remember. I was having a cup of coffee and watching people. A man walked by me with a shirt that said, "Good Shepherd." I went over to the desk and wrote a note on the chalkboard to the attendant. He nodded, picked up the telephone, and wrote back to me. I thanked him. He motioned for someone to come help me.

I got into a taxi with the note he had written and was taken to the address he wrote down. He had instructed the driver to wait for me and bring me back to the airport. When I entered the building, a woman came to assist me. I wrote on the chalkboard and she took my hand to follow her.

She said, "The name you have given me is of a dying woman. She has been here for three months with lung cancer and is in the latter stages of her life. The doctors have given her only one month or less to live."

I entered the room and lying in the bed was a tiny, elderly woman with grey hair who was blind in one eye. She looked at me confused. I stood there a little while and wrote on the chalkboard, "My name is Collette and I like to be called Collie."

She began crying and had the lady write on my chalkboard, "How old are you?"

I wrote my age down. She wrote, "I had a baby named Collette, she would be about your age. I was not married, became pregnant, and when Collette was born, I became very ill and had to give her up. I wrote the name Collette on a blanket and left her at a school."

"I am she," I wrote. "I was told someone placed me on some frigid, icy steps of a red, brick building. Did you put me there?"

"Yes, my daughter, I did!"

"Why, why didn't you keep me? Did you even know who my father was?"

She wrote, "No."

"Why didn't you keep me?" I asked.

She wrote, "I was extremely ill, had no breast milk or money to feed you, and had no one to care for either one of us. I waited, freezing in the bushes, until I saw someone take you inside. When I began walking down the street, I was crying so hard, I fell over and blacked out. When I came to, I was in a hospital with a high fever. I prayed for you many times over the years, that someone would come and adopt you, love you, and care for you better than I ever could. Did that happen for you, Collette?"

I wrote back, "Yes, Mother, it did happen."

She asked, "Can you ever forgive me?"

I wrote in return that I had already forgiven her. I leaned down and kissed her forehead and she smiled and squeezed my hand, forcing her lips to say, "I never stopped loving you, Collette."

I held up my thumb, forefinger, and middle finger over my forefinger along with my pinkie and signed, "I love you forever." I kissed her goodbye and left the nursing home, lamenting on the fact I had not known her until today. I prayed as I left, reminding myself that "the ways of the Lord are right," Hosea 14:9. I also knew that someday we would see each other again. At least His way was right for me and my mother at the time she had to give me up; otherwise I would have never met Isaiah and his family.

The taxi driver took me back to the airport. I was on my final flight to Fort Wayne.

Chapter 40

Sometimes I Love Lip Reading

Upon landing in Fort Wayne, I was met by Jeanna and Kevin and their two little ones, Zachary and Jessica. They looked just like their parents – how sweet they are. Kevin brought the car around and I was on my last journey back to the land and family I love! I hoped by not announcing my arrival by letter they will be excited to see me and want me to remain with them.

Jeanna signed, "Collie, if you have any reservations upon arrival, we will not carry your luggage into the house. We will make it seem like we are visiting and you can come back to Fort Wayne with us, until you decide what you want to do."

It felt so good when I got on the plane in California to be dressed in Amish clothing and comfortable shoes. I felt like I had never left the plain folks in this part of the country.

I was home at last! I did not need to be afraid of my reception as Rebekah, Deborah, Ruth, and Leah were home and cried and encircled me, squeezing and clinging to me as if I were going to disappear!

We were one hour away from lunch time when Rebekah signed, "Joshua and Isaiah will be coming in shortly. They will be ever so excited to see you as well. We welcome you home, Collie! You are planning to remain with us we pray. The weather is changing to fall and we have so many quilting projects to complete for the nursing home and other sewing projects as well, so please say yes."

Before I could even answer, the door opened and Joshua and Isaiah walked in. Joshua came to me and gave me a quick hug. Isaiah looked at me and I could see when I looked into his eyes he was pleased to see me. I also detected his hearing waning when Maem spoke to him. He took my hand, pulled me to him, and embraced me with an emotion I could not believe. I felt the tears well up in my eyes! I did not want him to ever let me go. He stepped back and signed, "My little shveshtah (sister) is home!" We sat down and ate lunch and Kevin and Joshua began talking.

Jeanna and Rebekah cleared the dishes and began washing them. Jeanna looked at me because the expression she saw on my face appeared to be startled when, once again, Isaiah called me "sister."

Isaiah signed for me to take a walk with him. While walking he signed, "Collie, are you going to stay with us, or do you intend to leave again?" At that moment I knew that even if he only saw me as a sister, I would still remain here.

"I will stay, Isaiah, I belong here! All of you are my family and I need to be with everyone who loves and cares for me!"

He smiled and signed, "You are very important to me, Collie, and when you left I knew for certain how much I would miss you. I would like you to remain and see if you can love me as I do you."

"I will remain, Isaiah, because I love you more than a broodah (brother), even though you see me only as your sister."

"Collie, when I speak of you as my shveshtah (sister), I mean you are my 'sister in Christ!' Not like Deborah, Ruth, or Leah, my blood sisters. Did you think that is how I thought of you?"

"Yes, Isaiah, I did think that is what you meant, when you signed it to me."

"Collie, I meant you are my sister in God's spiritual family. I could never think of you in any other way than being in love with you. I missed you so much and was afraid to write to you, because I thought you might have met and married someone in California. I love you, Collie, and have for many years. I was afraid to let you know because I didn't want you to have to spend your life caring for a man who cannot hear and is unable, sometimes, to help you!"

"Oh, Isaiah! I wanted to believe you would someday love me. I am so sorry we did not figure all this out before I left! I thought you were in love with Rachel and I could not bear to be here and watch the two of you spending quality time together."

Isaiah signed. "The important thing is that you are back and we will work it out together."

"I love you, Isaiah, and this is where I will always want to be, thank you!"

When we returned to the house, Jeanna took one look at me and knew I was going to stay. She smiled happily at us and came up to us placing her arms around us both. Isaiah thanked her and Kevin for bringing me home.

It was time for dinner and we all sat down to an Old Order Amish dinner of canned garden vegetables, venison, homemade bread, deviled eggs, salad, and lots of blueberry pie and coffee. I really liked being home and knowing I belonged with this family who always loved me unconditionally.

After dinner, Kevin, Jeanna, and their children began to make preparations to return to Fort Wayne. The children did not want to leave. Leah wanted to hold them all of the time they were here! All of the girls took them out to see the animals and Jeanna and Kevin allowed them to select a kitty to take back with them. We all laughed as Isaiah asked them if they wanted to name one of them Lokka.

When Jeanna and I were walking to the car, she signed, "I have never seen you so happy. You and Isaiah worked out your differences, didn't you?"

"Jeanna, if I would have never left and gone to California, Isaiah and I may have been married by now. He told me he loves me and I assured him I feel the same way about him."

"Collie, you and Isaiah have the rest of your lives together. Maybe you should marry soon and have a little one to raise and be ever so happy. This is what I want for you! You were never meant to be a city girl! You love the Amish life and living here. What a beautiful place to raise children!"

I signed, "You are so right about me not being a city girl. I thought I had to make a life in California until I read Rachel's letter. I will not push Isaiah, though! I want him to be sure that marriage is what he wants. He told me he loves me! You and Kevin are such dear friends and I will always be grateful to you both for seeing me through a lot of anxious and terrifying moments in my life. God is good, Jeanna! His plan for me is my heart's desire. I have been blessed abundantly!"

Kevin and family left about an hour later. Isaiah signed, "We should go visit Jacob and Sadie. They only live about three miles away."

So off we went! I love being in the buggy again and beside Isaiah leading the way. It is autumn in Indiana and the leaves are breathtaking. They have produced some spectacular color arrangements spread across the land. The trees in the woods and the openness of the fields and streams provide a gorgeous background that looks like an expensive painting. It makes me think of apple cider, apple butter, fruit pies, and all that is tasty.

I continue to look for apple orchards as we go along. Soon, it will be time for all the canning and baking. I look over at Isaiah and realize how much I love him. It makes me hurt inside to think I could have lost him forever if I had not received Rebekah's letter and found Rachel's in my luggage.

We arrived at Jacob's and Sadie's. They were outside working and smiled as we pulled in. Isaiah helped me down from the buggy and Jacob grabbed me and swung me around and around. Sadie hugged me and expressed with her eyes that she was happy to see me again. She is so pretty and they are perfect together! They have a lot of land to work and it is obvious they are enjoying each other so much.

I signed to Isaiah, "Tell Sadie I remember when she taught school for Lizzie Farmwald because she was ill for a while. Ask her if she is still teaching."

Sadie, in turn, told Isaiah to sign to me that after watching Anne teach, she decided to, also. Yes, she is teaching and is happy she got to know me when I was at the school. We went inside and had sassafras tea and homemade sugar cookies.

They were telling Isaiah some of the chores they were trying to get done and how many projects they had started. Isaiah signed to me as they talked. They laughed and I kept putting my hands to my mouth, so I wouldn't embarrass them with my gurgling sounds. We enjoyed our time together.

On our way home, I looked over at Isaiah. He had a slight smile on his face and looked quite content. I have always marveled at the degree of contentment and comfort we share in being together. Thank God that did not change after my long absence! I signed, "In the days and weeks ahead, I will tell you all about Hollywood, California, if you would like to know."

He nodded yes and I was anxious to tell him all about finally meeting my maem and that my brother, Bobby, and I got together. I believed he would be interested in hearing that! He will find that life strange compared to Indiana. Then, again, maybe he would prefer not to hear about it! I would know what to sign, when the time came.

He signed, "Our next visit will be to Joseph and Sara."

The following day, Rebekah, Deborah, Ruth, Leah, and I went to Shipshewana to shop. I was in need of more clothing and found the exact material.

Rebekah signed, "I will help you sew and you will have enough clothing for the winter months."

We then stopped at a small restaurant. We ordered chicken and noodles, salad, pie, and coffee. Oh, how I missed the homemade bread and peanut butter! I could have made a meal on that alone and enjoyed every morsel I could put into my mouth!

We returned to the buggy with all of our packages. An English couple approached us with a camera. We all turned our heads down and walked into another store until they went away. The girls giggled and Rebekah and I smiled as we watched them trying to cover their faces when we left the store.

We spotted the same couple going down the sidewalk, attempting to snap pictures of others who also kept their heads down. I guess they don't understand that the Amish do not want their pictures taken. We turned the corner laughing as Deborah walked right into Louis Graber. His face got beet red and we walked on ahead so she could spend some time with him. Ruth and Leah signed, "She is in love with him."

I signed, "You know, I believe he is in love with her, also! Look at the way he looks at her!"

Ruth signed, "Yeah, the same way you look at Isaiah and he looks at you, Collie!"

I smiled and walked on to catch up with Rebekah. We entered a bakery and looked over all the homemade breads, pies, cookies, and muffins. We purchased two apple pies and a cherry pie. We took our purchases and headed back towards the buggy. We saw Deborah and Louis laughing and gazing at one another, as if there was no one else in the world! Rebekah signed, "Come November, we will probably have another wedding." She sent Leah over to get Deborah.

All the way home Leah and Ruth signed, "It's a good thing you came back, Collie, or you would have missed another wedding!"

Deborah looked up with red face signing, "Whose wedding? Ruth and Leah, you are both of age. Have one of you met someone?"

Everyone laughed and Deborah finally caught on to us and signed to me over and over, "I am so happy, joyful, and singing from my heart!"

The weather was good, so on the way home we stopped at the home of Jonah and Erma Hursh to drop off the pies we had purchased. They were so glad we thought of them! Erma had been ill and not feeling up to doing a lot of baking. We told her we would come over and help her with more canning that needed to be done. This is what good neighbors do for each other!

After our evening meal, Isaiah and I walked around and held hands, quietly enjoying each other and the peace that is now between us.

Finally, I signed, "Today, I was reminded of the quietness and simple ways of this Amish life. I observed how self-expression comes in the form of woodworking, quilting, sewing, canning, and other crafts. I observed a young man whittling, and he was very good at his craft."

Isaiah signed, "We have an old saying, 'A man who trims himself to suit everybody will soon whittle himself away!'"

I squeezed his hand and smiled at him. He is forever teaching me! I love him so much! His humor is unexpected and ever so clever. In sign, he once told me, "A face without a smile is like a lantern without a light." I look back over my years and realize I was like that description. I now smile a lot and am looking forward to when Isaiah will ask me to marry him. I know I will have many instructional classes in becoming Amish. Being in his company has reminded me once again of the Amish ways. I have already accepted the dress code, lovingly so!

We left the next morning to help Erma Hursh, as promised, with her canning. Deborah and I rode in the backseat of the buggy. She signed to me, "Collie, Louis has already gone through Rumspringa and is baptized into the church. He has asked me to marry him. I have not told Maem and Daed yet, but I plan to tell them tonight. I wanted to tell you first. I am ever so excited! I love him and want to be his wife and have his boblis!"

I signed my happiness for her and Louis and will look forward to the wedding and helping with the plans.

As we continued our ride, looking at the fields, I thought about how young Deborah and Louis are. They will have many years and many boblis, God willing! I know Joshua and Rebekah like Louis a lot. He is a carpenter by trade, so Deborah will be well provided for.

Life is going by quickly and I also want to have a child or two someday. I sense Isaiah will soon ask me to marry him. I rode along with these thoughts and suddenly was startled and then fearful when a car came up behind us. A man honked for us to get over and zoomed around us recklessly. I will never get used to the rudeness of the English! Once again, I feel proud to be a part of the Amish and no longer consider myself English.

Chapter 41

Instructional Classes

Today is Sunday, but not a church week Sunday, so Rebekah and Joshua want us all to go visit families I have not yet seen since my return. That means we will go to Joseph and Sara's and then Amos and Rachel's. I am going to enjoy this day of visiting the family I haven't seen in a year and a half!

We brought pies with us for our three-mile trip to Joseph and Sara's home. Joshua, Rebekah, Leah, and Ruth rode together in their buggy, while Isaiah and I rode separately in his. We arrived just before lunch and were welcomed with hugs. Joseph and Sara were happy to see us and glad to hear I was home to stay. We visited with Sara and Rebekah signed our conversation. The men folk went to the barn to check out the various projects Joseph was working on.

The women folk cleaned up the kitchen and decided we had better be on our way because we had to go to LaGrange to see Amos and Rachel. If I had any reservations concerning Isaiah's acceptance of Amos and Rachel, I shouldn't have! He was so happy for them! Rachel immediately begins to sign to me, after she gave me a big hug. She was beaming with happiness and Amos looked like he had captured the best prize in the world!

Isaiah hugged them and signed to them, "My Collie has come home!" I swelled with self-esteem. After all of these years, I finally will have a mate who loves me. During my time in California, I never felt this way, with earthly praises and applause, like Christine did. Now I understand why she was happy there and I wasn't. The expression, "My Collie came home," resonated my whole being! God has been directing me and healing the wounds within me for a long time. He gave me the love of my life on earth in Isaiah.

Rachel signed, "Collie, let us take a walk and I will show you our land."

Maem, Deborah, Ruth, and Leah signed that they would prepare some tea and food for us all.

Rachel and I walked toward the fields and she showed me the deep rich soil that had grown their crops. She showed me the garden that would provide plenty of food for canning. The happiness glowed in her reflection of love for Amos and their land.

I signed to her, "When I got on the airplane to leave for California, I had forgotten to read your letter. I met a wonderful pastor who sat beside me on the plane. His name is Pastor Jack Webb, a magnificent man of God. We visited during the whole trip via writing on my chalkboard. We both had sore hands from so much conversation! He eventually became my pastor in Hollywood at his church, St. Paul Lutheran. Rebekah wrote to me about you and Amos and, I must admit, I was shocked! I thought you and Isaiah had married and possibly had a bobli by now."

She hugged me and signed, "Isaiah loves you very much. I saw it in him and you right after I arrived from Michigan. I was terribly jealous of you and unkind to you, Collie. I am so sorry! I thought if I spent more time with him and he less time with you, I would be able to get him to love me. Selfishly, this is why I wanted to learn sign language, so he would have to spend more time with me. However, I didn't count on really liking you. But, as time went by, things changed and I wanted us to be friends. Even after you left, I thought it would work to my good. Instead, he became more withdrawn and began to avoid us all. I wrote you the letter right away the night before you left, hoping that after you read it, you might turn around and come right back. I had no idea you took so long to read it.

"The importance of my telling you all of this is because I want to ask to be forgiven for the selfishness within me and the thoughts I carried against you and Isaiah's relationship – more importantly, for wanting to keep the two of you apart! I spoke to Isaiah before I realized I had fallen in love with Amos. I told him exactly what I am telling you and he has forgiven me. I pray you can as well!"

I signed, "Of course I forgive you. I have been forgiven in Christ over and over, how can I expect less for you?"

We returned to the house, both feeling cleansed, and sat down to a meal Rebekah, Deborah, Leah, and Ruth had prepared. The men were happy to be together as well. A father and two of his sons! What a bigger family we are becoming. I am so happy!

When we got ready to leave, Rachel signed to me, "Please come back as often as you can. Amos and I have missed you and we miss our family gatherings. Every Sunday is wonderful, but I wish we were closer so we women could quilt, sew, and just visit and enjoy one another."

Rebekah signed in return, "When we can, we will come back and visit. We want you to come and see us, also, so we can work on quilts for Deborah. Soon, we will have another wedding. After the harvest season, she and Louis will marry in November. That doesn't give us much time to get quilts made, so come often and help us. It is now the end of September and work is not as busy as a couple of months ago, so we will have more time for quilting and sewing. At next Sunday's church meeting at Jacob and Sadie's, the Amish communities will be told of the upcoming marriages."

On the buggy ride home, Isaiah was very quiet. He would look at me and smile, but we were very content in our silence. My thoughts were of the wedding preparations. We will have another person joining this loving family. This will leave Ruth and Leah at home, and both are courting local young men.

October went by so quickly! It is now time for Deborah and Louis's wedding! All of the plans are falling into place and the quilting is now completed for them to have four quilts added to the two Maem had saved for them.

Deborah was a lovely bride and they had so many people attend from all over the county. It was a day of praise and thanksgiving for all! The food was brought in from all over the District. Rachel, Sadie, Sara, and I relaxed and thoroughly enjoyed each other and the festivities. It was such a beautiful day, but rather chilly. The men made sure we were all comfortable and we thanked God for all of His blessings.

Deborah and Louis would travel around for the next few weekends, meeting new relatives and becoming reacquainted with old ones. Louis had built their home with some help from all of the men folk. He is a very good carpenter. He built a kitchen table with 10 chairs. He told Deborah they are for the godly number of children they will have. They looked ever so happy, and I thought soon the boblis will be arriving. They both want many!

When the following week arrived and we thought things were starting to settle down, Isaiah asked me to marry him! I was not prepared for his sudden announcement! I cried and in sign said, "Isaiah, I have waited 38 years to become a wife. I never thought it would happen. Yes, I will marry you and live happily with you until God calls us home. "Yes, yes!"

He wrapped his arms around me and held me ever so tightly. We were eager to tell Joshua and Rebekah.

Isaiah stopped before we entered the house and signed, "Collie, I may lose my hearing soon. I am noticing a difference lately and want you to know that you may have your hands full trying to help me adjust."

"My dearest Isaiah, we both have deafness we cannot overcome. You have enhanced my life from the moment you entered my signing class in Fort Wayne. We will work together to help you adjust. It will be more difficult for you than it was for me. I was born deaf and knew no difference! You will have to live with the memories of the sounds you once heard. Perhaps if we have a bobli right away, you will be able to hear his or her first cry and you can sign to me how it sounds."

He signed, "I would like that very much. Let us plan a wedding for next month, just before Christmas. Will that give you enough time to prepare? Let's go inside and see Maem and Daed and give them our announcement."

Joshua and Rebekah were not at all surprised. Isaiah, in sign, said, "Maem, will this be a burden on you and Daed so soon after Deborah's and Louis' wedding?"

Rebekah signed, "Isaiah and Collette, I have waited for this moment for many years! I knew in God's perfect timing, and if He meant for you and she to be together, nothing would stop it. We are going to contact everyone right away and you will have a fine wedding."

Joshua then spoke to Rebekah and she signed to us, "Collie, you have already become Amish in your dress, but there are other requirements you must meet to become of Old Order Amish, woman, and wife. After living around the Amish for a while and observing our customs and beliefs, you have done well! Now at church, every other Sunday, there are a total of nine instructional classes for becoming Amish. The ninth class is the baptismal service. You will join the church then."

Isaiah said to Joshua, "That means the wedding cannot happen for at least another four or five months!" I watched Isaiah's lips as he talked to his daed.

Rebekah signed to me Joshua's response. "You have both waited so long, my son, surely you can wait until the classes and baptism are completed. This is our custom! It will be May and a busy spring plowing and planting time for all of the families who may want to attend."

"Is there no other way Daed?"

"I have spoken, Isaiah," Daed said.

Throughout the night, Isaiah and I made our plans.

I signed to Isaiah, "I will have a lot more time to get quilts made and help with the chores. This will help Maem from being so exhausted because of all the weddings in her family. I am looking forward to being instructed in my confessions of faith, as I accept being Amish. I have never been baptized, and, once I am, you and I will be able to work in harmony under God as husband and wife. The time will pass quickly, don't you think?"

Isaiah signed, "Yes it will. We will work and play hard these next four to five months. Maybe you will go ice fishing with me come January and February. Remember years ago how much fun we had?"

"What an interesting layva (life) we will have together, Isaiah. You will have plenty of time to hunt these next few weeks, while I am learning my instructional classes."

"Yes, Collie, I will have plenty of time."

"Maem, Ruth, Leah, and I will can the venison and store it, so we can share in the bounty the Lord has provided. Do you remember telling me that in life it is in the giving, that we receive? I will be very busy with Maem making quilts for the nursing home again this year."

My instructional classes have begun. Bishop Samuel Nolt from a neighboring District is my minister throughout the classes. At night as I lay in bed reflecting on my first class of the articles I would learn, especially how God created the world, I tried to imagine woman made from the rib of man. Oh my, it is sometimes beyond me! The teaching went on to say how our first parents were driven out of paradise because of envy of the devil towards God. Deceitful as the devil was, and still is today and always will be, God promised us His son, Jesus, as the Christ-child who would redeem us with His life! I think how unworthy I have always been and how He gave His life for the sins of the world!

I cried before I went to sleep, asking God for forgiveness and help with the classes that make me sad one minute and so full of life the next. I shared all of these feelings with Isaiah.

"I, too, remember my confessions of faith, as I struggled so much with my unworthiness. Then I remember in John 1 where He tells us God is full of grace and truth. His grace is sufficient for us all, Collie, by His death on the cross and His resurrection from the grave. Daed is right: you will learn so much in these classes and feel God with you all the days of your life!"

In between my classes, I managed to not only study the Bible, but enjoy the many blessings of the family that are now so real and true to me. The wedding is getting closer! I often wished my mother could have lived to be here with us, but I am very happy and fulfilled I was at least able to meet her and hear her story.

Winter is now upon us. The cold weather and winds chill a body, I dare say! I like to walk and roam around the farmland and put my head to the sky to catch snowflakes on my tongue. How peaceful my life here will be! However, suddenly, the thought occurred to me: where will Isaiah and I live? Maem and Daed still have Ruth and Leah to wed. I will have to ask him, but it makes no difference, as long as were together!

We had our quilting bee yesterday at our home and sat around enjoying one another as we sewed. Leah and Ruth made rhubarb muffins and sugar cookies to go with our tea. How tasty they were! Ruth Hostetler told us, and Rebekah signed, "Love is a fruit in season at all times. Our hands can grasp it anytime."

The men returned from their hunting with another deer to take care of. Isaiah signed to me, "We will have to have a bobli boy after we are married because I will need a lot of help in the upcoming hunting season."

I was happy Isaiah was anxious for the wedding day to come. The thought of spending the rest of my life with him was all encompassing!

The flu season is back and we were all hit pretty hard. Joshua seemed to have it the worst. Perhaps his age is a factor now. I recalled that when I first arrived here, he had it then and often. Rebekah and I took turns with the cooking and placing cold compresses on Joshua's forehead to lower his fever. I was getting concerned for him that he may not get better when one morning his fever broke. He was finally able to have hot tea and small bites of biscuits. We were all very relieved!

Ruth and Leah also got the flu, as did Rebekah and I. Fortunately we did not get it all at the same time to render us unable to help one another until it finally subsided. What a nasty bug it was! Finally all of the laundry was caught up and we resumed our baking and canning. It was a time of loving care and caring for one another.

Isaiah came home today and signed, "Collie, they need a teacher for school tomorrow. The flu has hit hard and the teacher is sick. Miss Rosie has 10 children out with the flu. Leah can tell them what you sign and there may be only eight or nine children there."

Leah was excited and I was unable to say no. I enjoyed returning to the classroom again. A long time has passed since I taught! I remember Pastor Jack Webb writing a note to me once saying, "The Bible is our best mirror to see ourselves as God sees us." I was meant to be a teacher once, and now He is showing me I still can be! The most impressive part of the day was how Leah handled the children. She enjoyed the interaction and they enjoyed her as well.

On the way home I signed, "Have you ever thought about teaching?"

"Not until today," she responded in sign. "I enjoyed it so much! Will you help me find out what I need to do to pursue it?"

I signed, "Daed is the one who helped me, young one. You need to discuss it with him. I am sure he will be happy to advise you."

We taught the rest of the week and enjoyed every moment of it. Miss Rosie came back and was ever so happy at the lessons completed so she could continue on with no loss of time or subject matter. She also noticed the behavior of the scholars and the cleanliness of the classroom. She could not thank us enough!

Pork butchering began in early December. We will have a lot of pork, venison, and chicken this winter. Along with the vegetables and fruits we canned, our food supply should be plentiful.

With the November weddings past, there are two or three more this month. Soon we will be into the New Year and spring will arrive with May coming upon us fast. My confessional classes of faith will be ending and Isaiah and I will marry. Before that happens, though, I need to go to Dottie Landgraff"'s, because she needs a lot of help in her home. Her daughter married and lives far away.

Dottie fell and broke her right arm. Isaiah signed he will take me over to their farm and pick me up later. I will do some baking and her laundry. More than anything, right now she needs some visitors and encouragement. Some of the other neighbors and I will take turns helping. We will write notes to one another, as she is not able to use sign language. We manage quite well actually! Fortunately her right arm and hand are not the dominant ones, so she can do some things and not be in agony. I feel for her because she is such a busy woman and quite a seamstress. She quilts beautifully, but has trouble holding the material down with only one hand. I enjoy her company and she is quite pleasant despite her circumstances!

Rebekah signed, "Both Sadie and Sara are going to have a bobli. We are all so excited for them!" She also signed, "Jacob and Joseph are walking around happy and strutting like peacocks. It seems the boblis will both be born in late August or early September."

Rachel and Amos came to visit us a couple of weeks later. We wanted to share the good news with them, but they were already informed and happy. Rachel signed to me that she hoped her baby would be conceived soon. I hope they have many, because they are so happy together and want them while they are still in the early years of their lives. I thought of Isaiah and me. We are older than them and want a bobli very soon after our marriage, also. It is in God's good timing for all of us! I wished Amos and Rachel lived closer so we could spend more time together. Maybe someday we can have connected farms.

Amos signed, "We stopped in LaGrange on our way over here and one of the men folk told me a deer came down the street that looked like a six-point buck. He went to the window of a shop and bumped into it a few times. He didn't break it, then turned around and walked down the street to the corner and back toward the country road."

We all wondered why he did that and Daed said because he must have seen himself in the glass and thought it was another deer looking back at him. We all thought that was so funny! Amos signed they saw people standing on the street staring at him.

Amos and Rachel noticed the snow beginning to fall and decided it was best to leave before the roads got bad. Most were plowed well, but they didn't want to take any chances.

Rebekah commented that she thought she was getting a chest cold, so Ruth, Leah, and I made her stay in bed the next day. For the next couple of days we cared for her and did the laundry, cleaning, and baking. We made her chicken soup and hot tea with honey. She finally got on her feet the third day, but was very weak, so we all pitched in and let her rest and take it easy as much as possible. She was concerned that Joshua would get it, but he escaped it this time. We were so thankful!

Joshua asked Isaiah to sign to me, "A great writer by the name of Mark Twain once said, 'Few things are harder to put up with than a good example.'" He also said, someone once told him, 'Prayer is the place where burdens change shoulders.' We give our prayers and burdens to God. His shoulders are broad and He answers prayers. See, look at Maem. She is up and almost like a new woman!"

Chapter 42

The Marriage

This is the last Sunday for my classes on confessions of faith. My baptism will be at the last winter meeting. Winter has passed and spring is fast approaching. Easter has come and gone for another year. I am extremely nervous about our upcoming wedding! I have wanted this for so long and now am so nervous! It is only two weeks away! It is unusual to have a wedding in May, but, nonetheless, it is being carefully planned. Joshua has insisted we have it at our home here on the farm. There is plenty of room for all to attend and we will have the reception in the barn. It is agreeable to all.

Isaiah signed, "Collie, are you sure you do not want to send word to Christine and Peter and Jeanna, Kevin, and their two little ones?"

I signed, "I am sure. I do not want anyone to become more important on our day and have to worry about entertaining them. They will understand when I write them that this is our day. Am I being selfish?"

Isaiah signed, "Not at all! You are right, we would want them to feel comfortable with all of our families and friends and they may feel a little too English with our Amish ways."

I signed, "It is about us and our lives together here."

"Maem and Daed wish to see us together tonight to talk about something," Isaiah signed.

"Whatever could it be, Isaiah? Are they feeling okay, or is something really wrong?"

"We will find out tonight," he signed.

Joshua and Rebekah met with us. In sign Rebekah said, "We want you to have a choice where you will live. Isaiah, Daed is getting on in years and so am I. We built the Dawdy Haus for my parents, and on to the Dawdy Haus we built another. It has been empty now since your Grohs-mammi passed away several years ago. Daed and I would like you to tell us where you want to live. We still have Ruth and Leah to wed soon and they will go to their husband's families to live. Do you want the farm and the house and help Daed with everything, or do you want the Dawdy Haus or the other addition along with the farm in which to live? We still need your help around here, and, with both of you being hearing-impaired, and you going into total deafness now, Isaiah, we can watch over you as well."

Joshua spoke saying, "We need each other. Please, whatever you two decide will be of benefit to us, too."

Isaiah asked his daed to allow us to discuss it and answer them tomorrow. With that being agreed upon, we all went to our separate rooms to pray. How wonderful of them! I prayed. "Lord, help us make the right decision based upon your will."

The early morning brought more snow and very cold temperatures, at around eight degrees below zero. After breakfast, Isaiah signed to me that he would like us to look at the Dawdy Haus and also the addition that had been added on before we made a decision. We waited until the next morning and took the lantern with us to provide a little warmth as we went from room to room in each place.

We agreed the addition added onto the Dawdy Haus would fit our needs starting out. That way, Joshua, Rebekah, Ruth, and Leah could remain in the house and life could go on as usual. Isaiah told his maem and daed that he would remain, helping Joshua until such time Joshua would have to take it slower and easier. At that time, they can hire help if needed. He laughed, saying we could have many boblis and they also could help. Everyone seemed happy and pleased that things would remain the same!

Preparations for our wedding are right on schedule – everything being done by family and friends. Neither Isaiah nor I, or Maem and Daed, had to do anything. A special table was set up in the corners for the bridal party. I will sit to the left of Isaiah. The single women will sit on the right side of the room with me and the single men will sit on the left side with Isaiah. Rebekah, Joshua, and Isaiah's siblings will sit in the kitchen.

A second meal will be served just before sundown. Isaiah, Joshua, Rebekah, and I will sit at the main table and the same food will be served again. Our reception will go late into the night. The following day, the wedding will take place.

Isaiah and I were so happy to be joined as husband and wife. I will always remember how fast my heart was beating! Isaiah's hands were clammy and so were mine. I looked at Isaiah and knew I would reverence this man as my husband forever! The deep respect I have for him will give me confidence in his love for me as well.

Finally, our lives begin together and we are full of optimism about our future. I looked around the room tonight, our wedding night, and was happy to see Jacob and Sadie. She is getting big with their bobli. Joseph and Sara were here as well, and she also is getting big with their bobli. Amos and Rachel are still trying for a bobli in the worst way, but they are very happy together. Deborah and Louis, newly married, and all of us as a rapidly growing family, are all together. I am so pleased to have overcome many hurdles to be where I am today. "Thank you God!"

After we made the tour of all of the family and friends with thank yous and visits, we finally got settled into our home. Isaiah continued to help Joseph and I baked, did laundry, cooked, sewed, quilted, and adored my husband and married life! I often went to the house to help Rebekah with her laundry, and we would quilt together and talk in sign. We sat around the heated stove and the ladies who joined us to help would have Rebekah sign to me about the locals and English tourists and what they were up to. Life was all I wanted it to be and Rachel and

I both wanted to be with a bobli soon. Isaiah and I are the oldest couple in the family, so we better get busy or we will be too old to conceive!

As we neared another Christmas, we took about a dozen quilts to LaGrange to the nursing home. I always enjoy doing that, as everyone is so happy to receive them!

Spring has finally arrived and the flowers are coming up everywhere. Gardens are being planted and the fear of frost is over. This is a busy time for all!

Once again, the maple trees were tapped in February and March and we have a lot of maple syrup for the year. Most of the birds have returned and I am happy to see the tiny sparrows and the beautiful robins. Even though I have never heard birds chirping, cats meowing, children laughing or even crying, I can tell by their faces whether they are contented or unhappy. I am glad to be able to see God's creation return once again to our Amish farm lands. I really missed all of this when I was in California!

I decided to write to Peter and Christine.

"Dear Christine and Peter, Isaiah and I are married! We got married on May 21. I don't think you will be surprised and I trust you are not disappointed that we did not send out invitations. It was an Old Amish, traditional wedding and we had many relatives and friends from all over the countryside attend. I wanted to spare you the long trip for a three-hour wedding and late reception. Due to our customs, I would not have been able to spend quality time with you anyway, so it's best for all the way we did it. I know you are happy for us because of the many discussions we shared. Are you and Peter doing well? I imagine you are both real busy with your schedules. If you see Pastor Jack Webb, please tell him I am the happiest woman in the world! I will write to him soon. Please give Peter my love and tell him I am very happy and we miss him also! Do you ever hear from Bobby? Take care of each other and if you come back to Indiana, come and see us. We want you to know we will always make time for you! We love you my dear friends! Love in Christ, Isaiah and Collie."

I decided I had better write to Jeanna and Kevin, also.

"Dear Jeanna and Kevin, Isaiah and I got married on May 21. We are so happy and looking forward to a long life together. Maybe someday soon, we will have a couple of adoring children like yours running around our house. What a blessing to be married to this wonderful man whom I have loved for such a long time! We moved into the addition that was added on: the Dawdy Haus. It is quite large! Isaiah's hearing is failing and his maem and daed want us to remain close, so we can watch over one another. I would like to invite you to visit us this summer if possible. I am sorry we did not invite you to the wedding, but many families and friends were here from many Districts. The Old Amish wedding traditions prevailed and we would not have had any quality time to spend together. I am enjoying being in our home and have many things to do to keep me busy. We miss you, my friends, and look forward to seeing you this summer if possible. Love in Christ, Isaiah and Collie."

"Dear Collie and Isaiah, Peter and I are so happy for your marriage! We have prayed for this blessed event many times over the years. We are not offended by not attending the wedding and reception. What you have shared with me regarding the Old Amish Order belief system makes it understandable. The day belonged to you and Isaiah and you didn't need to be entertaining others! We will try to come see you next summer. This summer is full with another movie premiere. I know you understand how that is! You were such an intricate part in making our last movie successful! I have finally made it in the business I have loved since you and I were young and going to the theater in Fort Wayne! Peter is kind, patient, and very busy, and our life right now is all about us. I hope this is not being selfish on our part. Someday, we would like children, as well. By the time we make that decision, though, I may be too old. Right now, we are doing what we love and worked so hard to achieve. Give our love to Isaiah. Love you, Christine and Peter."

"Dear Collie and Isaiah, congratulations on your marriage! We are so happy for you! We understand why we were not invited to the big event. We have been to see you numerous times and know that this was your big day, with a lot of family and friends present. We are overjoyed that you are now married! You must have children soon so we can let our children get together, before they get much older. It sounds like the home you share is big enough for many children; although I know you would be happy with just one or two. We will try and find a couple of days to come and spend with you. We are glad Fort Wayne is so close that we can reach each other easily. Kevin is very busy, because it seems like crime is more prevalent now around here. I often fear for his safety! He is always careful and usually has a partner with him to investigate every call. I still worry, however! The children are doing well, healthy, and full of life. I am a very contented wife and mother. I know you are happy, too. We love you both and will see you soon! Love, Jeanna, Kevin, Zachary, and Jessica."

Chapter 43

The Baby

Several weeks have passed since the wedding and I am enjoying being married! All of the duties of being a wife are comforting to me. Our home is large and takes a lot of work, but that is okay with me! We need to fill it with boblis and are trying. Hopefully it will be soon! Isaiah is quite tired, as he is helping his daed and trying to help his maem as well. He also has all of our land to work. There is a great deal of work, but we both love it and our lives our content. Summer is coming to an end and fall is arriving soon. The harvest time will be extremely busy getting the corn and soybeans in. I have been canning all of the fresh vegetables and fruits. Ruth and Leah are helping as well, as it is a team effort. We are a large family, with many joyous hands that can accomplish a lot in a day! Oh such satisfaction to work the land! The Lord provides so well for us.

Amos and Rachel came by for a visit today. They appear to be quite happy! I thought she was going to have good news about a bobli, but not yet. She signed, "When God decides, we will be thankful and happy as can be."

We had a lovely time visiting and enjoyed a large dinner together. We laughed at one another's antics and stories signed. It is fun catching up on all the family and friends after such a cold and long winter and busy summer. It seemed we just got started visiting and it was time for them to leave.

After they left, Isaiah signed, "But godliness with contentment is great gain," 1 Timothy 6:6.

I smiled and signed, "Yes, Isaiah, a deep reverence for God. I am very contented."

A few days later I woke up ill. Isaiah asked Leah to come and check on me throughout the day. In sign he said to me, "The flu is going around again. Rest and drink lots of fluids today. The weather is changing and that is most likely the reason. Perhaps tomorrow you will feel better." I told Leah to tell Daed to stay away from here today!

I drank some chicken broth Leah had prepared and was unable to keep it down. By the time Isaiah returned from the fields, I was retching so hard I could barely lift my head! "I believe I have a fever," I signed.

Isaiah placed his cool hand over me and signed, "You must stay in bed tomorrow as well. I will have to take you to the doctor if this continues. For now, you must have fluids!"

The next morning I woke up feeling a little better. He went to the fields to work and I sat up and almost passed out! Rebekah came to check on me and made some toast, crackers, and tea. They helped considerably and, by mid-afternoon, I was up and sewing, feeling much better. It returned again two days later and I began to think something terrible was wrong! Isaiah took me to the doctor in Shipshewana. He told Isaiah I am carrying his bobli!

We returned home and Isaiah went back to the fields to work. I went down on my knees and thanked God for our child within me! I prayed for good health for the child and myself and thanked Him for the blessings He is giving us.

Over the years, my life has been filled with twists and turns. But, as always, God is in charge. His plans for us will surely be fulfilled! I signed, "God, please let our child be born without my disability. If you so choose, let me deliver the bobli with no problems. No matter what happens, we will cherish this child and give him to you. God, if I am not being too bold, I would love to be able to give Isaiah a child who is normal and not like me."

Isaiah, at the same time, was out in the field working and thinking about the child within me. He began praying, "God please give us a healthy child. God, if our child is deaf (or a deaf-mute), we will adjust to her or his plight in life and help all we can to make life as easy as possible, so he or she will get along well in the world. I do ask you to make this child just like his mother. Collie is the most wonderful person I have ever encountered. Her handicap has only enhanced the gifts you have provided her. She will be the best mother anyone could ever want. I ask that you keep Collie sound and healthy throughout her pregnancy. Thank you God for my life and the life of our child to come."

Every family member was happy with the news of the coming bobli. Isaiah and I laughed over the numerous baby items being knitted, crocheted, and sewn. It appears everyone intends to spoil our bobli, no doubt. Maybe he or she will become a teacher. Maybe a master craftsman. Maybe, if we are blessed with a boy, he will become a Bishof (Bishop) or farmer!

Rebekah came by today and we had tea and her wonderful molasses cookies. She is so excited for us and wants to help as much as she can. I am so happy!

We are, once again, in winter and now it is cold. Isaiah brought a lot of wood into the house and shoveled a wide path from our home to Maem and Daed's, in case we need them or them us. I am unable to do a lot of lifting now because our bobli is getting big within me, so I have trouble bending down and getting back up. Still, I will never complain about this bobli!

The snow is so bright, but, without electricity, the home is very dark. The lanterns are lit in the middle of the day now, yet it is still somewhat dark. I feel the discomfort of the wind on such overcast days as these. I am unsettled today and my heart is heavy with grief over our church family member's loss.

I learned today that one of our church families lost their 28-day-old grandson. He had to go to a big children's hospital in Indianapolis, Indiana, but he didn't survive. His family belongs to the Old Order

Amish Church. I will grieve for them and pray they will be able to have another child someday when the time is right. Isaiah did not want to tell me, but he knew I would feel badly if not told. I will pray for everyone, that is why he wants me to know. We will bake some things and Isaiah will deliver them. Hopefully he can deliver, as the weather is not good and no one is visiting. In fact, we have been unable to attend church at Joshua and Rebekah's home. I am looking forward to them having the service there again!

Isaiah went ice fishing today with his broodah (brother), Joseph. They were like two little boys fishing together. Hopefully, we will have fresh fish for supper tonight. They are both good fishermen. Sara came with Joseph to spend some time with me. We visited, baked, and walked the path to visit Maem and Daed. I invited them to come for fish and fresh baked apple pie, too. Daed can never resist the offer of pie of any kind! I showed Sara the clothes I have been sewing for the bobli. She went to her bag and brought back a few items she had made, also. She loves to crochet and made several pair of booties, a blanket, and a hat. I got excited touching all of the handmade clothes, knowing my delivery time is just around the corner.

In the next day's mail, I received a package from Christine and Peter. They sent more homemade booties and cloth diapers. I was so happy to hear from them, and they, too, are excited my due date is very soon. I smiled as I opened a picture frame for our bobli, as she forgot we don't take pictures. Oh well, I will make use of it somehow. Maybe the first picture colored or drawn by our bobli will be placed in the frame. Isaiah shared how precious their friendship is to us.

"Dear Christine and Peter, the last few days are giving me spring fever. The temperature is above freezing and the snow is melting fast. Ice is still around in some places, but not as bad. Isaiah is hauling skubala (manure). I remember on the airplane going to California, Pastor Jack Webb was asking me many questions about the Amish way of living. I told him Isaiah had been hauling manure. He laughed at my response. He is such a wonderful man! Isaiah is also filling the wood pile again as we will need it for some time yet. I was sure I saw the winter wren at the bird feeder last week. I also saw a couple of bluebirds flying around the bird houses. The milder temperatures are very welcome.

"Maem had a sew-in at the main house. It is amazing what so many hands can accomplish! We enjoyed being together and visiting as we worked. There were 16 of us, with many stories to be told. I liked the one that was signed to me, 'The true measure of life,' I am told, 'is not its duration, but its donation!' Some of the family's children this winter have had chicken pox and whooping cough. I am thankful we in this household are spared during my carrying time! The sap will soon be rising and the dreariness of winter will be gone for another year.

"We have some neighbors a couple of miles down the road who gave us some more lard from the large sow they butchered. What delicious pies they will make! They also shared with us some canned meats. We are surely blessed! We wish to thank you for the gift box you sent. Our bobli will look precious in the booties and the cloth diapers will come in handy. We pray you are both feeling well and know you are busy with your careers. We miss you! Write when you can, and come visit soon. Love in Christ, Isaiah and Collie."

Chapter 44

He Can Cry

On March 16, 1997, our son was born. Caleb was 21 inches long and weighed seven pounds, eight ounces.

"We shall call him Caleb," Isaiah signed. "Joshua of the Bible blessed Caleb and gave him Hebron as his inheritance, because he followed the Lord, the God of Israel, wholeheartedly. He is so beautiful, and he can hear, Collie! He can cry!"

What blessed news that was! We thanked God and Isaiah gave him over to God, to do what He must to make Caleb the man He wants him to be.

I signed to Isaiah, "I am now 40 years old and my childbearing days are most likely over!"

"Collie, I will never need any more than what God has given me. You and my son Caleb fill my life to the fullest."

"Caleb's life will not be as miserable as was mine in the different foster homes. He will not have to endure mocking, jokes, laughter, and, yes, Isaiah, even torment and tricks at the hands of other children because of my disability. We have been blessed with a precious son, who will make his way in our world, normal as any other boy, meeting all the challenges a normal boy encounters. However, he will not be worldly."

"We must give our thanks to God," Isaiah signed. "I am now 42 years old and am happy with our one child. We will enjoy him for as long as the Lord allows. He will become a fine carpenter, just like Joseph taught Jesus. We are surely blessed!"

Caleb grew strong and what a delightful little boy he was to have around! He had several kittens he would carry with him and Isaiah decided he needed a dog. "Every boy needs a dog," Isaiah signed.

How afraid that dog was of everything and everybody! She was a combination of Cocker Spaniel and Labrador. Her eyes were really dark and she had very dark eyelashes. She looked like she was wearing makeup. Isaiah called her "Sissy," because she cowered around squirrels and rabbits like they were going to chase her if she looked away.

What a gentle nature Sissy had. She was perfect for Caleb! He could punch her nose, pull her hair or ears, and step on her tail, but she never tried to bite him in return. In fact, she would only jump and run in another direction. The perfect pet! Caleb followed Isaiah around the barn, in and out of the house, about two steps behind him all of the time. And Sissy followed Caleb the same way! The three of them formed a line as work was being accomplished. I smile and thank God every day for the twinkle I see in Isaiah's eyes when the three of them come into the house.

The years flew by all too quickly. In fact, we recently celebrated Caleb's seventh birthday! I was never able to conceive again, but we are so happy with our son that it is all right! He loves school and has many friends. His teacher, Miss Leah King, as well as his aunt, told Isaiah that Caleb does everything he is told to do and is quite intelligent. I already knew this, as he learned sign language and was very proficient with signs when he was only three. By the time he turned five, we were communicating very well!

Joshua and Rebekah always enjoy his visits, and when he walks into their house, they always have cookies and milk waiting for him. Grohs-mammi lets him gather eggs with her, and that is their special time together. Grohs-doddy lets him feed the chickens and work with him in the barn, teaching him how to work with wood.

Amos and Rachel come by more often than the other siblings. They still have not been able to conceive! I understand Rachel's frustration, but someday it will happen and she will be a good maem. "Maybe they are trying too hard," Isaiah signed. They certainly enjoy Caleb and he is always excited when they come to visit. He loves going to church and sings really loud and not always on key, but his heart is into it! We all laugh about that! I pretend I can hear him when he laughs and mouths the words.

On Monday, Isaiah left to go into town and Caleb wanted to go with him. Isaiah signed, "I would love to take him, Collie, but I have to stop at the feed mill and want to talk to Eli Miller about something. Is it okay if I don't take him today?"

I distracted Caleb by taking him to Grohs-mammi's for a cookie. The weather is so beautiful and we walked to the barn to see Grohs-doddy. He gave Caleb a ride on the pony and cart. He was laughing and yelling because Grohs-doddy was, too.

Just then, a buggy pulled into the drive and Isaiah's youngest brother, Joseph, and his wife, Sara, and their child got down from the buggy. We were delighted to see them and right away Caleb wanted to run around with his dog, Sissy, to show them what a clever dog she is. Sara's son, Tyler, was older, but he went along with Caleb, laughing at him and Sissy's antics.

A car then pulled into the drive and a man walked up to us. I saw Joshua turn away as he was speaking. Rebekah looked at me with a startled expression and began crying. Everyone began crying! I tried to scream with no sound coming forth! I knew, I knew! Joseph wrapped me in his arms and I pulled away with my hands flapping uncontrollably.

I looked at Rebekah again and she signed, "Isaiah was hit by a truck! The truck was trying to pass him and, in order to avoid hitting a car head-on, the driver chose to go back into his lane, hitting Isaiah's horse and buggy. He said Isaiah never knew what hit him."

The man went on to say that Isaiah never heard his horn and he died instantly. I may have had a scream come out from the depth of my being, because I could not catch my breath and I saw everyone put their hands to their ears, including our Caleb.

Isaiah had signed to me a long time ago that funeral practices vary with our Districts, but some things reflect our Amish values, like simplicity, humility, and the community aid given to our families. He was always so wonderful teaching me his way of life!

Our family and friends took over all of the farming and household chores and even watched Caleb. The funeral arrangements were planned, food prepared, and accommodations were made for all of the horses and carriages. Isaiah's body was taken to the funeral home and, within a day, returned to his parent's home. He was placed in a simple pine coffin on a bench. Wall partitions were removed for better viewing of the speaker.

For two days, family and friends from all over visited our home. In a nearby cemetery, a grave was being dug by hand. A simple hour-and-a-half service was done with hymns sung, Scripture read, and the Bishop preached a sermon. The buggies then lined up for the funeral procession to the cemetery. Caleb and I were in Joshua and Rebekah's buggy. A horse-drawn hearse led the procession down the dirt road. Behind, a long line of Amish carriages kept pace.

Upon arrival at the cemetery, everyone climbed out of their carriages and tied their horses to the hitching posts. Isaiah's coffin, supported by two poles, was carried to the open grave and placed over it. Long straps were placed around each end of the coffin and the pallbearers lifted it with the straps, while another man removed the supporting cross pieces. The coffin, containing my beloved Isaiah, was then lowered into the ground and the long straps were removed. The pallbearers shoveled dirt and began filling the grave. When each shovel of dirt fell to the casket, I watched my husband, the man I had loved and wanted, put to rest. I cried and cried and realized I would never survive this day if it wasn't for our son. Our close friends and family members returned home for a meal. I sat stunned and held Caleb tight to me, until I could breathe normal again. I was told later Isaiah cried out "Collie and Caleb" before dying!

One month later, Peter and Christine arrived. I started to visit with them, but was unable to concentrate on our conversation. They were enraptured with Caleb! He has been so good for me these past few weeks. He seemed to understand the depth of my grief and I concentrated fully on him.

Christine signed they would have to be leaving to return to California, but will keep in touch with me. "If you and Caleb need to move back with us, we will make room. We would love to have you both!"

A week later, Kevin and Jeanna came with their children. They were extremely sad for us all. They want Caleb and me to come to Fort Wayne and visit, when we feel up to it. I told them I would consider it. I also told them about the offer from Peter and Christine, but already know I do not want Caleb growing up in that fake Hollywood atmosphere. How easy it is for people to want the glamour, money, and power Hollywood offers! But that life is not for Caleb. He will be like his daddy and the heritage he inherited!

The next month, we lived with Kevin and Jeanna for a while. With so many changes, I needed for us to get away and find a way to cope and raise my beloved son alone.

Six months have now passed and Caleb and I are still in Fort Wayne. I have enough money Isaiah left us, but I am missing our family in Shipshewana.

I haven't felt well since Isaiah's passing, so I went to the doctor today. He ran a lot of tests and Jeanna came to tell me I have an appointment to find out the results. She went with me to review the results and discuss them with me. The doctor said, "I am sorry to tell you, Collie, but you have stage four breast cancer!"

Jeanna signed to me what he said and I asked, "What does that mean?"

"He wants you to take chemotherapy and radiation, Collie. The cancer is rapidly advancing and he wants you to make a decision soon!"

"What should I do, Jeanna?"

She signed, "Let's pray about it and we will call him tomorrow."

We did pray and she signed to me everything the doctor told her.

I signed, "Can you and Kevin take Caleb and I home? I want us to be back with our family. I have felt sorry for myself long enough! No treatment will help me. We need our family now. They are filled with such love for us, so we will go back."

Caleb is now eight years old and so much like his daed. Such a loving boy! Amos and Rachel were the first to see us since our return. We have become an even closer family since Caleb's birth. I love them dearly!

I was in bed one evening reflecting on all that Isaiah had signed to me over the years. "Collie, you must agree to become plain." I wore the plain clothes, because this is the life I have chosen. Rebekah had given me her dresses to wear and took me shopping for shoes. In her busy days, she took time to teach me housekeeping, cooking, Bible reading, sewing, and quilting, and Isaiah taught me Dutch before joining the church. I even thought of the nine weeks of Bible instructions and the day of baptism and how nervous I was. Hymns were sung and sermons were preached before the baptismal rite took place. When the Bishop called the candidates to come forward, my legs were shaking so hard, I thought I couldn't walk. We were all told to get on our knees. Isaiah signed to me what the Bishop was saying. He asked me, "Can you confess that Jesus Christ is the Son of God?" Along with the others, I signed, "Yes, I believe." The Bishop then poured water he had cupped in his hands onto our heads and baptized us. I realized then that I was no longer English, but Amish! I was placed in full fellowship with all rights and responsibilities of adult membership. I was so proud! I had become plain and I would be free to marry Isaiah, hoping he would ask me soon – and he did! As I reflected over all of this, my confirmation, Isaiah's love for me then and now, I knew what I had to do.

Joshua went to LaGrange the next day. The following day, Amos and Rachel came by. I signed, "I want you to raise Caleb for Isaiah and me, because I do not want him to grow up like I did. At one point I would have given my life away, just to be held by a stranger, I so wanted to be loved. He has that love here, now, and forever. Will you let him become your son? I am not going to live much longer, as the battle with cancer is taking me soon."

We all cried and they signed they were honored I had chosen them for my son. They would love him forever and never let him forget his real parents.

I had Caleb come into the bedroom and signed to him. "I have a letter I want you to read from Pastor Webb. I met him on the airplane going to California. I have mentioned him to you in the past."

"Dear Caleb, when I was traveling by airplane back to California, I met your mother. She is an amazing person and loves our Lord and Savior with her whole being. Seated next to her, I observed her reading a lot. She read many letters from your Amish families giving her encouragement, support, and love. I am writing to encourage you to continue on having that same love for the written Word of the Lord that she has.

"I would like to offer you an opportunity someday to come to California where I reside and be educated in the ministry alongside me at St. Paul Lutheran Church in North Hollywood, California. Of course, we will wait until you turn 18 or older if you should decide to come. In the meantime, if I am able to be of any help to you, and you want to contact me at any time in the future, I have enclosed my address. God's blessings to you son. Pastor Jack Webb, St. Paul Lutheran Church, North Hollywood, CA 91605."

I watched Caleb as he was reading the letter. He began to cry. He agreed to be raised by Rachel and Amos and signed that he loved them, but he wants me to stay with him. Knowing that I cannot be with him, he reluctantly agreed to also consider Pastor Webb's offer someday, but he might never want to leave Indiana. I signed that it will be his choice. Selfishly, I hoped he would remain with his Amish family. He promised he would be a good boy for his daed's family. Then I signed, "Let us give thanks to God for each other."

My last request is that I be buried next to Isaiah. I want the service to be like his, plain and simple.

A few days later, as my time was drawing near to join Isaiah, Amos and Rachel came into the bedroom. They had a small-sized tombstone to be placed on our graves with my approval. Written on it in sign was "I Will Love You Forever." The sign for "I love you" was placed below it.

When Rachel and Amos returned from the funeral, their life with Caleb had begun. In life, I had been given justifying grace and God's redemption through the blood of the Lamb. Now, in death, I am experiencing life's highest purpose. Being with my Lord and honoring Him with praise and thanksgiving, loving Him forever without any handicaps.

Perhaps Caleb will choose to remain in Indiana Amish country, but perhaps not.

CPSIA information can be obtained at www.ICGtesting.com
Printed in the USA
LVOW041025191212

312345LV00004B/12/P